MW00618115

ARCHANGELS

Rise of the Jesuits

Janet M. Tavakoli

Published by Lyons McNamara LLC, Chicago, Illinois.

Library of Congress Cataloging-in-Publication Data:

Tavakoli, Janet M.

Archangels / Janet M. Tavakoli

ISBN-10: 0-9851590-2-2

ISBN-13: 978-0-9851590-2-3

Also by Janet Tavakoli

Non-fiction
Unveiled Threat: A Personal Experience of Fundamentalist Islam and the Roots of Terrorism, Lyons McNamara LLC, (2014)

Credit Derivatives & Synthetic Structures, John Wiley & Sons (1998, 2001). Also available in Japanese and Orthodox Chinese.

Structured Finance & Collateralized Debt Obligations, John Wiley & Sons (2003, 2008).

Dear Mr. Buffett: What An Investor Learns 1,269 Miles from Wall Street, John Wiley & Sons (2009). Available in English, Orthodox Chinese, simplified Chinese, Japanese, Portuguese, and Turkish.

The New Robber Barons, Janet M Tavakoli (eBook compilation of articles from the 2008 financial crisis to January 2012).

Coming Soon
Archangels: Rise of the Jesuits Companion – Non-fiction eBook

Archangels 2: Vatican Gold- Fiction

The Money Book – Non-fiction: Tavakoli pierces the fog and predicts what you should buy and sell to take advantage of global financial turmoil and when to shift your investment strategy.

Note to Readers

This is a work of fiction, a product of the author's imagination. Characters, banks, corporations and organizations, if real, are used fictitiously, with no intent to describe their actual conduct, except for instances in which documented historical events are referenced.

When control of the Vatican is at stake—money talks and nobody plays fair.

Italian intelligence specialist and former Jesuit student Michael Visconte is shocked by the brutal murder of a Jesuit priest, who turns out to be a hedge fund manager for the Vatican. The victim, Father Matteo Pintozzi, achieved an unblemished record of extraordinary returns.

The next day, Michael is visited by two Jesuits who ask him to investigate the murder, and Michael soon finds himself in the middle of a struggle for power and control over the finances of the Vatican. Unfortunately, his lucky break— one that should provide critical evidence—blurs the line between good and evil and not only endangers the lives of Michael and the Jesuits, but also imperils the lives of his wife and children.

Table of Contents

Also by Janet Tavakoli

Acknowledgements

Acknowledgements

I would like to thank the many people who offered comments, encouragement, and suggestions. In particular, I would like to thank Kenneth Brian Brummel who reviewed an early draft. Libby Fischer Hellmann and Diane Piron-Gelman gave generous encouragement and editorial advice.

I would also like to thank Father J. Allan Meyer, M.D., Nancie Poulos, Rita Ilse Guhrauer, and Pamela van Giessen.

CHAPTER I

Vatican City
Saturday, June 15, 2013

Helena Visconte first saw Father Matteo Pintozzi when he stepped out of the sacristy into the deserted curved colonnade that led to the Vatican museum. She had no way of knowing that within a few minutes the priest would arrive at his destination, and both their lives would change.

By now tourists would normally be milling about, but a fluke June thunderstorm had just ended, leaving a vaguely musty smell rising with the vapor from the hot stone pathway. Father Pintozzi glanced to his right and then to his left and looked relieved, as if he were grateful no one was in sight. He quickly swept past the Vatican courthouse, the Eagle fountain and the Papal Academy of Science.

Her three-year-old son Luke took advantage of her distraction, gave a yell of unbridled glee, darted from behind the pillar and ran headlong into the flowing folds of the Father's black cassock. Helena was hard on his heels. She approached Luke from behind, crouched down, and grabbed him by the arm, pulling him away.

"Forgive my son, Father," she apologized in Italian. "He is overexcited this morning." She straightened, turned towards the priest and stood transfixed, staring at him. She brushed her thick auburn hair away from her face to see him better.

He looked young and virile, not more than thirty. His dark curly hair, huge brown eyes, sculptured Roman features and full sensual lips made him resemble a dark Apollo come to life. The graceful drape of his cassock, cinched with a purple sash, hinted at a well-formed body underneath.

She noticed he was aware of her stare. His eyes flashed with life and intelligence, and with a spark of amusement. He knew the impact of his looks, and she was sure he was gently mocking her.

She tried to recover her composure. "Your blessing, Father."

He gave the barest hint of a nod, bowed his head for a long moment and then raised it again. His earlier playfulness had vanished. He looked solemn, yet peaceful. Helena bowed her head and gently touched Luke's hair as he imitated her gesture. "*In nomine Patris, et Filii, et Spiritus Sancti*," Father Pintozzi said, making a graceful sign of the cross. "*Amen*." His blessing wasn't rushed but Helena noticed him shift his weight as if he were eager to leave.

"Thank you Father." She watched him hurry away. He walked like a trained athlete, his stride energetic yet graceful, his back strong and straight.

**

A few more steps took Father Matteo Pintozzi out of the Vatican into the streets of Rome. He looked around to make sure he was out of sight of the mother and son. Satisfied, he strode past some closed banks and gelaterias. With the thick slanted high wall enclosing the Vatican on his left, he followed the twisting path up the Viale del Vaticano to the entrance of the Musei Vaticani.

Although the museum was not scheduled to open for another five minutes, he pushed through the door. He stepped inside, once more on Vatican soil.

He looked up as he ascended the spiral ramp, just as everyone did. A twentieth century addition to the museum by Giuseppe Momo, Father Pintozzi's art historian friends dubbed it "the DNA" because of its double helix shape. The ramp suited the museum, adding to the anticipation of entering the largest, and most valuable and comprehensive collection of classical art treasures in the world.

But Father Pintozzi's feeling of anticipation had nothing to do with art. His heart thudded gently in his chest, and beads of sweat formed on his temples and upper lip. He looked down the curving ramp but saw no one. Still, someone could be hugging the shadowed walls, out of his sight. He heard nothing either. Of course, he wouldn't if they didn't want him to.

He came to another door at the top of the ramp, and his hand trembled as the door slowly swung open in response to his pressure. The museum was immense, its chambers and alcoves filled with paintings, mummies, statues, furniture and frescoes.

Moving more cautiously now, he passed through the vestibule. He needed no map; he knew this palace of art as well as he knew his childhood home. He ignored the staircase on his left leading to the Sistine Chapel and walked out to a small open-air courtyard. For a moment he turned to his right and gazed at the dome of Saint Peter's Cathedral, which overlooked the lusciously groomed Vatican gardens. The gardens looked serene and empty, as if they were enjoying a few moments of peace before the hordes of tourists descended.

Pintozzi passed through another closed corridor and then into the open courtyard of the Pigna with its incongruous modern-looking globe of brass.

He walked through the long marble corridor of the Chiaramonti Wing, filled with busts and statues of Greek and Roman gods and nobles. As always, he imagined the statues subtly moving to greet him as he passed. He belonged here. He wondered if he looked like one of them, a chiseled piece of black marble come to life.

His tension lifted. He loved the sound of his sandals slapping on the marble beneath his feet, the comfortable coolness that radiated from the smooth stone. Most of all, he loved the absence of people.

He paused for a moment to take a breath before he arrived at his destination, the Braccia Nuova, the new wing. After he dealt with the transaction to occur, he planned to see Father Herzog, the head of the Jesuits. He needed to persuade the Superior General to help him.

Father Pintozzi opened the final door, and the impact of the familiar sight beyond made him step back a pace. The yawning gallery was filled with shadowed niches, each of which contained an ancient marble statue on a pedestal. Ancient mosaics in the marble floor depicted scenes of Roman daily life. The towering ceiling was embellished with carved rosettes framed by fluted squares that led up to skylights.

He was late, but he saw no one as he scanned the room. No one, he thought, except Julius Caesar, Augustus, Demosthenes and other ancient personages who stared at him from their respective alcoves.

His sandals made a soft scraping sound on the marble as he came to a stop. He paused, and then walked around the eight foot statue of the Nile river god that reclined against a small sphinx. He stood in a twelve-foot semicircular area that couldn't be seen from the main hall.

He waited and listened, but he still heard nothing. A minute went by, then another. His thoughts wandered. Father Pintozzi knew every dark sin the Society of Jesus was hiding. He knew most of the Vatican's other secrets as well. Which was why he needed Herzog's help. He knew he had made mistakes. He knew he was under suspicion. But once Father Herzog understood the situation, Pintozzi was sure the old priest would help him make everything right.

Pintozzi barely noticed the soft whisper of air behind him. A shimmer of silver passed in front of his eyes, gone almost before it registered. "Traitor," someone hissed.

The priest's eyes widened. He recognized the voice. He was about to say something when he felt a pinch, followed by a cut, as a thin wire sliced through the soft flesh of his neck. He felt blood pumping in spurts from beneath his chin, a spreading wetness. He felt more confusion than pain as it cascaded down his cassock and spilled onto the floor.

He slumped to his knees, his body no longer under his control. He fought for breath, but choked as he inhaled foamy red liquid. As he crumpled onto his side, the cool marble floor felt like a soothing hand against his cheek. Colors deepened, then vibrated and danced. He watched a thick red pond ooze over the small triangular patterns inlaid in the floor. Pintozzi wondered whether the mosaic was porous enough to be stained by his blood. A shame if it were.

Above him the statue of Pallas Athena, goddess of wisdom, gazed down at him from her alcove. She seemed to be laughing. *Yes*, he thought, *I haven't been wise at all*. He tried to laugh too, but the remaining air in his lungs bubbled up in a death rattle. Even that didn't prevent him from smiling at the irony. He had made a mistake. It was all a ridiculous mistake.

He realized he had only seconds left and summoned all his willpower for the Jesuit test of consciousness. His last conscious intent would be for the benefit of his killer. In silent prayer, he gave his final absolution: "I forgive you."

Pallas Athena grew dimmer, and a profound weariness overtook him. She was calling him to go back, or was it to come? *Yes, I'm coming,* he thought. *I'm coming, but slowly, since I am so very tired.*

CHAPTER II

Rome
Saturday, June 15

Michael was dreaming. After all these years, he knew he could will himself to wake. The problem was he didn't want to.

Irena's rich golden hair glinted in the sunlight, and she smiled as he held her. She was just as he remembered her: young, vital, and charming. She lay on the picnic blanket where they had just made love, her petite frame covered with the blue cotton dress she carefully laundered and pressed every day. Suddenly he felt cold and alone, filled with dread. She moaned and a pool of blood spread across her legs and stomach. He tried to scream her name, but all he could manage was a shrill unrecognizable sound. The sound came again, then again. Belatedly, he recognized it and groped toward his bedside table.

"Michael?" a distressed female voice asked as he groggily put the phone to his ear.

"Helena?" Michael nearly said Irena, before recognizing his wife's voice. "What is it? Is something wrong?"

"Where were you? The phone just rang and rang." Helena sounded irritated as well as anxious.

"I was sleeping off the effects of that cold medicine you gave me."

"Oh, I'm sorry." The strain in her voice was stronger now. "I need you to come here as quickly as possible. I just found a body. A priest. In the Vatican Museum. Someone killed him."

Instantly alert, Michael kicked back the covers and got out of bed.

"Where are you?"

"In the museum cafeteria. At a pay phone; I didn't bring my cell. Luke's with me. I took him to see the Sistine Chapel—"

"Helena," Michael said urgently, "did you see anyone, anyone at all? Did anyone see you?"

"No. No one."

"Where did you find the body?"

"Hold on a moment. I need to check the map." After a long pause, Helena spoke again. "In the Braccia Nuova in back of the statue of the Nile, where it opens up to a little internal courtyard. The statue blocks the view from the main hallway."

His mind raced as he gave her instructions. "Helena, listen carefully. Don't leave the cafeteria. There must be tourists getting breakfast. Find the busiest, most visible area and stay there."

"You don't think there is any danger, do you?" Now she sounded worried.

"Let's just play it safe." He tried to sound reassuring. "I'll be there as soon as I can."

"All right. And Michael?"

"Yes?"

"I love you."

He hesitated. Then, "I love you, too."

CHAPTER III

Vatican City
Saturday, June 15

Rome has several kinds of policemen.

The Vigili Urbani are the elegant traffic cops seen in the piazzas doing their ballet of traffic direction in a futile attempt to bring order to the chaotic Roman traffic. They wear white helmets, navy blue trousers and white jackets. They are mainly for show and for parking tickets.

The Polizia, deal with the usual crimes of the big city: drugs, murders, rapes, prostitution, thefts and domestic disputes. The Polizia wear navy blue suits.

The Carabinieri deal with terrorism and international crimes, and they are technically part of the Italian army.

Michael's group had no name, and belonged to none of the others. The Carabinieri and the Polizia called them the Specialists. An American would call them spooks. The Specialists were Italy's version of the FBI and CIA combined. They also handled sophisticated cybercrime and financial crimes. For decades they had been fruitlessly investigating the links between a rogue faction of the Catholic clergy calling themselves "Archangeli," and the Mafia. It was the most frustrating investigation in the history of their division.

Michael knew he shouldn't barge in; he had no jurisdiction. The Italian government and the Pope had signed the Lateran treaty in 1929, making the Vatican the smallest sovereign state in the world, less than half a square mile in area. This meant that either the Swiss guards or the Vatican guards should be handling this inquiry.

But this was his wife and his son, and their safety was at stake. And it was the first big break he'd had in a seven-year long investigation. He headed it and was authorized to call the shots. He'd deal with the fallout later.

Michael's apartment was only five minutes from the museum. He arrived at the crime scene eight minutes after he hung up with Helena.

He knew he wouldn't find out anything once the Vatican authorities arrived. The Vatican was under no obligation to file a report with the Roman police. They could quietly bury a priest without any autopsy, and that would be the end of it. There was no time for notes; he'd have to work quickly.

He looked down at the corpse, twisted in the agonized death spasm of a man starved for air. The priest had apparently bled to death. Michael guessed the man had been dead for less than thirty minutes.

He rested his palm on the priest's black curly hair and gently tilted the head back. The slice through the neck looked like a Mafia-style garroting, clean and professional. Death would have come swiftly.

The staring dark brown eyes looked almost alive. The face was surprisingly peaceful, which made the lump of flesh protruding between the lips all the more ghastly. The man's genitals had been cut off and stuffed in his mouth. Its corners turned up slightly, as if he were engaged in a pleasant conversation. As if the atrocities inflicted on his body had not touched his mind. Only that desecration and the whitish-grey pallor of his skin betrayed his horrible death.

Michael walked around to the other side of the body. He didn't flinch as he pulled back the cassock and examined the genital area. There was negligible bleeding around the excisions. The genitals must have been removed post-mortem.

Three sets of hands grabbed him and pulled him roughly away from the body. Vatican guards, from the glimpse he got just before they smashed him down on the marble floor. His chest hit the ground so hard, it knocked the breath out of him. He heard a cracking sound as his nose and forehead struck the floor. His ears rang, and he felt disoriented.

"What do you think you are doing?" one guard bellowed, pulling Michael's head up by his hair. The guard's other hand grasped Michael's wrists in a vice-like grip, forcing his arms uncomfortably up his back. Another guard pulled out a cell phone and stepped to the side to make a call. He spoke quickly and then rejoined the others.

Michael tried to shake his head to clear it, but the hand grasping him by the hair held him fast. Resisting would make the situation worse. Anger made him ache for combat, but he reminded himself that he was the trespasser. The guards were just doing their jobs.

He took a breath and concentrated on speaking. "I'm a Specialist. I found this body." He kept his voice calm, knowing that the guards were totally out of their element. As best he could from flat on the floor, he assessed the three men. They looked to be in their twenties and no doubt they were well trained. Individually, Michael could have taken any one of them, despite his 36 years. Possibly two. Three would have been difficult, but just last year Michael had faced down three men and came out the victor. He never should have let them sneak up on him.

The oldest-looking guard, who was also the shortest, did most of the talking. "Why were you touching the body?"

Michael kept his mouth shut.

"Who are you?" the guard demanded.

"If you free my arms, I'll show you my ID."

The senior guard kept Michael on the floor and searched him for weapons. Finding none, he allowed Michael to stand up and extract his card.

Even at six foot one, Michael had to look up at the Vatican guards. The shortest of them was easily six foot four. Michael handed over his ID, then pulled a white linen handkerchief from his breast pocket and attempted to halt the flow of blood from his nose. Combined with the congestion from his cold, he felt miserable.

The leader of the guards examined Michael's ID. "Michael Visconte. I've heard of you. You head the Specialists." His statement was part accusation, part admiration. He eyed Michael's nose with a trace of apprehension.

"Yes."

"What were you doing here?" The guard glanced at the corpse, his expression grave and sad. This was apparently something beyond his experience, and Michael guessed he wasn't sure how to proceed.

"I'm an art lover," Michael said without a hint of sarcasm.

"Why didn't you call for help as soon as you found the body?"

"I was trying to figure out what happened to him." Michael knew the guards had to be forceful, especially since he had disturbed the crime scene. Something he never would have done outside the Vatican, but here the rules didn't apply.

"You were looking up the man's ass for clues?" another guard burst out. He sounded more nervous than angry.

Michael nodded toward the body. "See for yourself."

The three guards studied the corpse in horrified fascination, gaping at the contents of the dead priest's mouth as they just now took in the awful details.

"Know him?" Michael asked.

No one spoke for several seconds. Finally the senior guard said slowly, "I didn't know him well, but he was a Jesuit."

An important piece of information to give away, though none of the guards appeared aware of that. Michael knew they were well trained, recruited from the best of the Italian army, but it was likely none of them had ever seen a murder victim before. This wasn't the typical Vatican purse snatching they were used to dealing with. They kept looking to Michael as if for guidance.

He addressed the senior guard. "Perhaps I can be of assistance."

"We don't need your help." The guard's tentative tone betrayed his lack of confidence. He upped his volume: "We've had anti-terrorist training."

"What makes you think a terrorist did this?"

The senior guard abruptly looked towards Michael. "Who else could have done it?" His voice wavered.

Michael said nothing.

The senior guard questioned him for a few more minutes and wrote down Michael's ID information, but didn't ask Michael to file a report. Michael was turning to leave when he felt an odd sensation, as if someone was staring at him from behind. A chill raced up his spine. Then someone spoke. A male voice, deep and resonant.

"Is this the man?"

Michael turned and saw a powerfully built man assessing him. He wore casual golf wear and carried a black bag. The short-sleeved shirt revealed muscular, hairy arms. The left one sported a diamond-studded Rolex. Michael knew this man must be the doctor, but he didn't approach the body. Michael guessed the man's question had been about him, not the corpse.

"Who are you?" the doctor barked.

Before Michael could answer, the senior guard spoke in a deferential tone. "Father Graf, he was here when we arrived. He's with the Specialists. His name is Michael Visconte."

Father Graf looked Michael over as if he were a piece of furniture out of place.

"Father Graf, are you a Jesuit?" Michael asked. For a doctor to be a priest as well was rare. Among holy orders, only the Jesuits commonly included members with training in prestigious lay professions.

"You can go now," Father Graf said.

"I'd like to stay while you examine the body."

Graf moved toward him, pugnacious as a bulldog. "You are not needed."

His hostility made the hair rise on the back of Michael's neck. Was Father Graf going to hit him?

"A word of advice, Mr. Visconte," Father Graf continued. "This is Vatican business. It's dangerous to forget that."

Michael met his gaze. "Thanks for the advice. Believe me; I'm in no danger of forgetting anything."

He felt Father Graf's eyes on his back as he retreated down the corridor to find Helena. By now the entire wing had been closed off. A petite woman with light reddish hair was trying to get through the barrier, claiming she was with the press. She looked familiar. He turned around, trying to get a better look at her, when a German tourist complained about not being let through and tried to push past the barrier. Two guards approached the German from behind and led the man away.

Michael gave up on the red-haired woman and decided he'd better leave. He strode through the halls, noting the increased number of guards among the sightseers being allowed to finish their browsing everywhere but in the Chiaramonti Wing. More tourists milled around the museum's entrance, glum-faced at being denied entry. As people exited, the guards examined their bags and purses. A few people were pulled aside and questioned, but Michael was certain the guards would learn nothing.

He rushed back through the same courtyards the dead priest must have walked through two hours earlier. The sun had burned off the haze from the early morning rain, and it promised to be a hot day. Michael glanced at the dome of St. Peter's, on his left as he hurried past. It was crowded with the distant, tiny doll-like figures of tourists.

He walked straight ahead for a hundred yards, then turned left and went down the flight of stone stairs to the museum cafeteria. He found Helena and Luke sitting with a group of German tourists. A ragged smear of blood stained one side of Helena's dress, its reddish-brown color stark against the yellow silk. The sight brought back his early morning nightmare, with a jolt of panic that he fought to control.

Helena looked over at him then, and Michael motioned for her and Luke to follow him onto the terrace. Attached to the cafeteria, it overlooked the Vatican gardens and had a partial view of St. Peter's. All of the tourists were busy getting a quick breakfast before their museum tour, so the terrace was empty.

While Luke explored amid the tables and chairs, Helena put her arms around Michael. Her head came only up to his chest, and she buried her face there. He gazed down at the mass of fragrant hair curling down her back. She looked tiny and vulnerable.

"What took you so long?" She looked up at him, a stricken expression in her almond-shaped, amber eyes. "Michael, your nose!"

"I was detained for questioning. The Vatican guards were... a little enthusiastic. I got here as soon as I could. Are you and Luke all right?"

She nodded. Luke came up close to her, and she took him by the hand. "We're just shaken up.

But what about you? The guards...did they hit you? Did you get into a fight?"

"No, of course not. I'd never give them a hard time in their territory." Michael attempted a reassuring smile. "It was just a misunderstanding. They were doing what they were trained to do."

"Is your nose broken again?" Helena persisted. "There's blood on your collar."

"It will be fine. I'll have someone look at it later." The swelling and congestion was actually becoming painful, but it was just a temporary inconvenience. He wouldn't see a doctor; he never did for anything this minor. "Helena, tell me again what you saw."

"Right now?"

"Yes. While it's still fresh in your mind." He reached into his jacket pocket and took out a notebook and pen. He had learned long ago that human memory was notoriously unreliable. The Specialists had a rule, like physicians: if it wasn't properly documented, it never happened. Michael would record his own notes after taking Helena's.

Helena took in a long breath. "Well, it's odd. Luke and I ran into the priest minutes before I found his body. Or, rather, Luke ran into him." Helena pulled the squirming three-year-old a little closer.

"Where?"

"Just off St. Peter's square. I brought Luke to see it before our tour of the Sistine Chapel. That's when Luke bumped into him. The priest gave us his blessing. He wasn't dead then, of course, and I got a good look at him. I knew it was the same man the instant I found his body."

"Did you notice anything unusual?"

"No. Just that he was in a hurry."

"Did you see anyone else, anyone at all?"

"No one."

"What happened then?"

"As soon as the museum opened, I bought our tickets and a map. I wanted to get inside before the tourists started arriving, because Luke can be a little hard to handle."

As if to prove her right, Luke broke free from her grasp. Helena lunged for him and pulled him back to her side. "Oh, no you don't, I'm not letting you out of my sight again."

"You were going to the Sistine Chapel?" Michael interrupted. "The Nuova Braccia isn't on the way to the Chapel."

"I know." Helena shot him a guilty look. "Luke ran away while I was buying the map. He made a beeline for the Chiaramonti Wing. I guess the long straight corridor attracted him. When he saw me trying to catch him, he ran to the end of the main hall and made a right into the Nuova Braccia. I couldn't keep up. He's too fast for me, and my high heels slowed me down. I was afraid I'd slip; those marble floors are so smooth."

Michael looked down at her shapely legs supported by stylish Italian leather shoes with three-inch heels. He smiled inwardly. Helena still surprised him. She was usually so sensible, but she was also fashionable enough to spend a day touring a museum in shoes like that.

Helena followed his gaze and stopped at the stain on her dress. "I suppose you'll want this for evidence. I got some blood on my hands and forearms, but I scrubbed them in the women's room." She shivered. "I couldn't stand the blood on my skin."

"You did everything right," he said soothingly, and kissed her cheek. "What happened then?"

She drew a breath and sighed. "When I got to the entrance of the Nuova Braccia, I couldn't find Luke. I called out for him. I walked into the center of the wing and looked behind the statue of the Nile. That's when I saw the body."

"So Luke wasn't with you?" Michael couldn't suppress a worried frown.

"No. Luke never saw the body, thank God. The Nile statue blocked it from view. I backed away from behind the statue, and suddenly Luke appeared further down the corridor."

"Was anyone else in the corridor?"

She shook her head. "Luke and I were the only people in sight the whole time."

"I saw somebody!" At Luke's unexpected shout, Michael and Helena exchanged a look of alarm.

Michael bent down to Luke, who squirmed in Helena's grasp. "Who did you see?"

"A man. When I ran in the big room, he hid behind a statue. I thought he wanted to play hide and seek."

"Did the man see you?"

"I don't know. I guess maybe. I ran to where I saw him and looked behind the statues. Then Mommy called me, so I hid behind a statue just like the man did. I wanted her to find me, but she didn't play." Luke looked at her accusingly.

"What did the man look like?" Michael asked.

Luke's face puckered as he thought about it. Then it smoothed out and Luke beamed. "Like a priest."

"What do you mean like a priest?"

"You know. He had priest clothes." Luke looked at Michael as if his father were a little slow.

"Did you notice anything else about him?"

"He had a briefcase. Like yours, but rounder."

Michael made his voice as calming as he could. "Luke, I want you to think hard. Take your time. Describe the man's face."

Luke frowned as if in thought, but Michael could see his three-year-old was at a loss. Finally, something seemed to come to him, and he grinned. "He had a priest's face, like them." Luke proudly pointed toward a group of priests inside the museum cafeteria.

Michael gave him a hug. "That's fine, Luke. Now do Papà a favor, okay?"

Luke nodded.

"Don't tell anyone about this. Don't speak to anyone about it, except me. Not even Anthony."

Luke nodded again.

Michael released him and let him run to the far side of the terrace, then moved to block the exit door. Helena followed. Once Luke was out of earshot, Michael spoke. "Describe the body to me."

She looked at him quizzically. "He was young, probably in his late twenties. He seemed to be in very good shape, although it's hard to tell much with him wearing a cassock. He was about six feet tall, dark brown hair and eyes. He sounded like a native Italian."

"You spoke to him?"

"Just briefly. We first saw him outside the museum, near the Papal Academy of Sciences. He gave us his blessing. He spoke Latin, but with an Italian accent. Then he went on his way."

"How long was it before you found him?" Fresh anxiety gripped Michael. If the killer had been tailing the priest, he would have followed Helena too.

"Not long. He must have entered the museum just before it opened, a few minutes before Luke and me."

"And how did the body look when you found it?"

"His neck had been cut. Right through the trachea and the carotid artery. There was a lot of blood everywhere." A small sigh escaped her.

"Are you sure he was dead when you found him?"

"Don't *patronize* me. I know a corpse when I see one."

Michael didn't reply. Conversations with an edge were becoming a familiar pattern in their marriage.

Helena continued more gently. "I checked a couple of pulse points just in case, but he was definitely dead."

Michael nodded. Helena had taken an emergency medical course before their first son, Anthony, was born and a refresher before Luke came, and she never flinched at the sight of blood. As a witness, she was reliable and competent. He felt a surge of admiration. Few people would have had the presence of mind to do that well in a crisis.

"Did you notice anything else, anything unusual?"

A flash of humor danced in her eyes. "Isn't a corpse in the Vatican Museum unusual enough?"

"Not quite," Michael said. "Did you notice anything in his mouth?"

"In his mouth?" She paused. "No, there was nothing in his mouth. I opened it to see if his airway was clear. His windpipe was severed, his neck clogged with blood. He wasn't breathing. He was still warm—he couldn't have been dead more than a few minutes—but I knew it was hopeless. Nothing could have revived him."

Michael mulled over what she had said. Finally he asked, "How long did all this take?"

"Just a few seconds. I knew he was dead the instant I saw him. I just wanted to be sure, in case there was a chance. And I was worried about Luke. I still hadn't found him." She searched his face. "Do you think the murderer saw us?"

"I can't be sure. But he was almost certainly hiding while you were in the Braccia Nuova. Probably in an alcove behind a statue in the Main Hall. He wouldn't have been able to see you unless he peered out from the alcove and risked being spotted. But he is one bold killer. That much I know."

"How do you know he was there the whole time?"

"Because he tampered with the body after you found it."

"Tampered with the body? How?"

Michael told her. The shock and horror on her face made him regret it.

"Michael, this seems like *La Cosa Nostra.*"

"Possibly."

"You promised…"

"I know. But we're already involved."

"No." Helena's voice cracked. "You can't do this. You promised me you wouldn't. Not after what happened to Marco and his family." She went rigid, her gaze at once demanding and searching.

Michael returned her look. After a pause, he said, "You're right. I'll find someone else to handle the investigation. But I still have to ask a few questions."

"We can't be involved," Helena insisted. "You promised we'd get away from these people."

Michael simply nodded.

"Think of our children," Helena said softly. "I want them to have a normal life."

"I'll turn this over to someone else as soon as I can. In the meantime, leave the dress at home and do not have it cleaned."

Helena gave him a dissatisfied glance, then turned away. He knew she was thinking of all the times she'd heard his vague promises before. "Watch Luke for a moment. I'll be right back."

Before he could stop her, she disappeared into the crowd. Michael scooped Luke up in his arms and scanned the throng. He couldn't see Helena. Then she reappeared, the blood-stained dress draped over her arm. She thrust it toward him. "Here. You can keep it. I never want to see it again."

She stood before him in her slip, heavy silk in a yellow and red paisley and flowered Florentine pattern. Despite the situation, Michael almost smiled. Even on a hot day, Helena always wore a slip when they were in the city. Her world was one of standards and the proper way to do things. The slip almost worked as a fashionable silk shift; she looked like a stylish Milan model. It was just a little too revealing, though.

He took off his suit jacket, removed his cell phone and wallet, and draped the jacket around her shoulders. "You'd better wrap this around yourself when you walk out of the museum." He ignored her anger. He knew it was her way of covering fear and nervousness. This wasn't the time or place to discuss his leaving the Specialists. He focused on what they needed to do next.

"I want you to take the children and go to the villa at Ostia. Take the nanny, the maid and the cook. You'll have to stay until it's safe to come back to Rome. I'll come out tomorrow night, but I'll stay in Rome during the week."

Helena nodded, looking worried again. "What will you do now?"

"I think it's time I talked to a priest." Michael folded the dress until it formed a neat square, hiding the bloodstain. Then he escorted his wife and son from the museum.

***

The Red Brigade terrorist activity in Rome had been halted, but Mafia terrorist activity had not. Helena was right, Michael thought; this murder smacked of Mafia involvement. The Specialists had some old books on the Vatican Bank scandal dating back to the early eighties, a few carefully worded blurbs in the Roman papers and a few decades-old articles in *Euromoney*.

Michael went to his office and spent the next three hours sifting through the files the Specialists had prepared over the past thirty years. The familiar facts were as grim as ever. The Mafia had long since infiltrated Italy's political power structure, and investigators risked their families' safety as well as their own. Italy's top Mafia-prosecuting judge, Giovanni Falcone, along with his wife and two bodyguards, had died when a bomb exploded on the road to Palermo in May of 1992. The Mafia used cell phones to communicate, and they patiently waited five days for their chance to kill Falcone.

A month later, magistrate Paolo Borsellino followed his friend Falcone to the grave after his car blew up outside Palermo; the five policemen riding with him became his companions in the morgue. The bomb was a gift from the Sicilian Mafia. Mafia thugs were investigated for the crime as late as 2008, yet investigators still didn't have a clear story and no one was prosecuted. Borsellino's family claimed it was a State murder.

In May of 1995, chief investigator Giovanni Tinebra and his family narrowly escaped death when their house was bombed. Tinebra was lucky. He and his wife were in the bedroom of their sick child when the bomb went off. The family fled the building before flames engulfed it.

Killings, beatings, kidnappings and threats... these were the Mafia's staple for solidifying control. They seemed immune from prosecution. Michael counted 62 good men who had met their Maker in Mafia attacks during the past two decades. For him personally, last year was the worst. His closest friend and colleague, Marco Tomba, was killed along with his pregnant wife and three-year old son. Forced off the Amalfi road by an SUV. Marco had skidded for 200 yards in a desperate attempt to save his family before plunging over the roadside precipice. The car bounced five times, then landed as a mangled lump of metal 150 feet down the mountainside.

Law enforcement and magistrates weren't the Mafia's only targets. They went after anyone they found inconvenient. Like Roberto Calvi, murdered thirty years ago, a crime for which no one had yet been held accountable. The book on top of the short stack by Michael's elbow held all the lurid details, but after seven years of digging into Mafia secrets he didn't need to read it to refresh his memory.

Roberto Calvi was head of Banco Ambrosiano when it collapsed in 1982, its depositors the victims of massive embezzlement with the Vatican Bank's complicity. Calvi was part of the scheme and fled Italy with incriminating documents. He was later found hanging under Blackfriar's Bridge in London, along with his expensive watch, $15,000 in cash in a variety of currencies, and a false passport. British authorities pronounced the death a suicide, despite the impossible acrobatics necessary for Calvi to dispatch himself that way and the presence of pharmaceuticals in his hotel room sufficient to produce a quiet, painless death.

In 1998, Calvi's remains were found by chance in a cupboard at Milan's Institute of Forensic Medicine. The Italian courts ordered the remains re-examined using the latest forensic techniques. Medical examiners proved Calvi was murdered, but the remains were so decomposed that they couldn't determine the exact cause of death.

In December 2002, a Mafia supergrass named Antonio Giuffre told police that Mafia bosses murdered Calvi out of anger at his mishandling of their money. More indictments came in August of 2003, this time of leading figures in Rome's underworld, but those too came to nothing as Calvi's murder trial dragged on for twenty months. In the summer of 2005, Licio Gelli—another officer at Banco Ambrosiano—was indicted for Calvi's murder. Michael, just beginning his own investigation into the Mafia and the Vatican, had seen the arrest as a spark of hope, but reality soon set in. Gelli used his connections—to Banco Ambrosiano, to the Mafia, and to the P2, a secret society of right-wing Freemasons—to evade all responsibility for Calvi's murder and for the embezzlement scheme. He testified at trial that Calvi's execution was ordered in Poland for his alleged financing of the Solidarity trade union at the behest of Pope John Paul II.

The crowning debacle came in June 2007, when Judge Mario Lucio d'Andria claimed the evidence against the defendants was insufficient. He threw out the charges, saying the real murderers were either dead or not in the courtroom. The acquittals were confirmed in 2011.

Michael's nose was throbbing and his head ached. He grabbed the books on the Vatican Bank scandal and stuck them in his briefcase, then left his office. Nothing said the murder of the luckless priest had any connection to a thirty-year old crime, but where the Vatican and the Mafia were involved, Michael had learned to take nothing for granted.

CHAPTER IV

Rome
Sunday, June 16

Michael woke up frustrated and irritable. After finishing his review of the files, he'd spent the rest of the previous day trying to find someone in the Vatican who could tell him about the murdered priest. The Vatican radio station made no mention of the murder. Michael's persistence finally drew a terse official comment from a Swiss Guard: "Father Matteo Pintozzi, age 28, orphan, money manager for the Society of Jesus, native of Naples."

Society of Jesus. That at least was something. The guard he'd spoken to earlier in the Vatican Museum had told the truth when he said Father Pintozzi was a Jesuit. Money manager was an important position, albeit an unusual one for someone so young. Many of the Jesuits turned over inherited wealth to the Society, and they allowed the Society to use and invest their earnings. The Jesuits seemed obsessed with wealth management. Though what—or if—that had to do with Pintozzi's murder, Michael didn't know.

Helena called to say she and the boys were safely installed at the villa. "Everything's fine," she told him. He could hear the determined calm in her voice, her attempt to reassure him as well as herself. "I brought the house staff from Rome, and the gardener and the caretaker and his wife are here, too." She laughed a little. "I've told everyone to be on the lookout for strangers or anything out of the ordinary. You don't need to worry about us; just take care of yourself." He'd promised to do so, then rung off feeling slightly better. But only slightly.

***

Michael decided a morning run would ease his frustrations. His cold symptoms had vanished, and his nose felt nearly healed. He'd placed an ice pack on it for over an hour, and only a little residual soreness remained.

It was only 6:30 but the temperature was already 85 degrees Fahrenheit. He stretched, then ran along the road leading to the Castel Sant'Angelo. A massive bronze statue of the Archangel Michael crowned the huge second-century circular building. The statue was a new addition, relatively speaking, and more than two hundred years of Roman weather darkened the bronze. Michael felt a touch of gloom as he approached. The black angel with its distended wing span and drawn sword evoked the Angel of Death.

The Castel itself likewise prompted dark thoughts. It had been built as a mausoleum for the emperor Hadrian. The crypt was bathed in centuries of blood. It had served alternately as a fortress, a barracks and a political prison. Puccini even saw fit to have his opera heroine, Tosca, hurl herself from its battlements.

He reached the Castel and made a left onto the footpath that wound around the west bank of the Fiume Tevere, the Tiber River. The early morning sun glinting off the water made it appear silver. Fortunately, the Tiber, unlike most European rivers, was relatively clean.

The temperature along the river was a few degrees cooler than the rest of Rome; but it wasn't long until hot air began to burn Michael's lungs. He stripped off his cotton running shirt and tied it around his waist. It was already soaked with sweat.

After a couple of miles, he turned right to cross the Ponte Milvio. Once over the bridge, he turned right again to run back along the east bank of the Tiber. When he reached the Ponte Sant'Angelo, he made yet another right onto the bridge and closed the loop for his run home.

The bridge had statues of St. Peter and St. Paul on either side, each accompanied by five large baroque marble angels designed by Bernini. As Michael ran across the bridge, he looked at the top of the Castel in the distance and saluted his dark archangel alter ego.

Just up the road, a hundred or so feet from him, Michael saw a young woman. Her long golden hair reflected the early morning sunlight. A slight breeze gently rippled the skirt of her simple blue sundress. She looked familiar, and he realized she resembled Irena as she appeared in his dreams.

As the woman stood looking out over the river, a young man emerged from the shadows of a pillar along the promenade. He wore a black shirt and black pants. He grabbed the girl's purse. She held onto it, and they struggled. Then he struck her, and Michael saw the glint of metal in the sunlight.

He sped up, unwinding his shirt from his waist. As he reached them, he swung the shirt toward the assailant's knife hand and rammed his right fist into the side of the man's head. The man turned just enough so that Michael landed only a glancing blow.

Michael was surprised the thief had anticipated his move. The man took a step back, whirled around, and sprinted away.

Michael was about to pursue him when the woman grabbed his arm. "Wait, I need your help!"

He looked at her in alarm. "Are you hurt?"

"No, but…" She clung to him in desperation and Michael felt warmth rise in him despite already being hot from his run.

"Wait here." Michael gently extricated himself from her embrace, then sprinted off after the assailant.

The thief was surprisingly fit. Given long enough, Michael could run him down, but just barely. He saw the man turn down a side road and redoubled his speed. The attacker was nearly a hundred yards ahead, the gap closing but not fast enough. The man rounded another corner and Michael heard a motorcycle roaring into action. By the time he turned the corner himself, a second man had joined the purse thief. Both were speeding off on the bike, one man driving and the attacker clinging behind him.

Michael gave up the pursuit and walked briskly back toward the young woman. He thought of her embrace and how it made him feel. She had seemed so grateful and desperate. He wanted to protect her. But when he reached the bridge, she was gone. He looked down neighboring side streets, puzzled. No sign of her.

His frustration came roaring back. First no word on the dead priest, and now he'd failed to apprehend a criminal. The victim had disappeared, so no complaint would be filed. Maybe she thought he wouldn't return. Or she was badly frightened and simply wanted to get away. He'd file a routine report on the incident, but there was little to go on. For the second time that morning, Michael resigned himself to defeat.

***

Despite the purse-snatching incident, the run had taken the edge off Michael's nerves. Exercise always had a calming effect and made him feel focused and alert. He drank two large glasses of cold water, toweled off, and turned the air conditioner up to maximum. He wanted the luxury of cold.

Next he lifted weights and did some abdominal work and stretches. Finally he took a cool shower and dressed in slacks and a smooth cotton shirt. He fixed himself an espresso with a breakfast of sliced peaches and whole grain cereal. Helena had taken the cook with her to Ostia, but he really didn't mind fixing his own meal. He was grateful for the privacy.

He sat down for a few moments and read *La Repubblica,* Rome's daily paper. Then he looked at the online version and also perused the *Rome Sentinel*. There was nothing about the murdered priest. He wasn't surprised. The Vatican had ways of suppressing embarrassing news.

Next, Michael skimmed the online editions of the *New York Times*, the *Wall Street Journal*, the *Herald Tribune, Handelsblatt, China Daily,* and the *Financial Times*. More talk of the downturn in the German economy and probable strengthening of the dollar as money fled to relative safety in a crumbling global economy. He would have to give some more thought to shifting around his investments this week.

Although he loved his work with the Specialists, there were times when Michael wished he were managing more than his private inheritance. Just as he put aside the newspapers, his doorbell rang.

He walked down the hallway to answer. The inlaid Italian ceramic floor tiles were too slippery for his two young boys, so Helena had created a path with a red silk Sarouk runner. Michael thought the strip of carpet looked like a welcome mat for the guest he was about to greet. An unexpected conviction came over him as he neared the door that the person behind it was already in the room with him. With each step, the air grew a little heavier and warmer. Strange... and stranger still that he simply accepted this, as if it was the most natural thing in the world.

He opened the door, and the feeling grew overwhelming. A draft of warm, comforting air seemed to envelop him. The man who stood before him looked around sixty years old. He was five feet ten inches, wearing a priest's collar and a black suit. Black, wavy hair with silver-grey streaks and tufts of silver at the temples swept back from the newcomer's face in a thick mass, almost touching the collar. His light olive complexion had the rugged look of long exposure to the elements.

Most of all, Michael was captivated by the priest's eyes. A deep blue, almost violet, they looked at him with a knowing gaze.

"Good morning," the priest said in accented Italian. "I hope I am not disturbing you."

"No, not at all." Michael couldn't tear his gaze away. "I just finished breakfast." Even as he spoke, he had the feeling that the priest already knew this.

"My name is Paolo de Aragon," the priest said. "I was wondering if I might have a few words with you in private."

"Of course, Father de Aragon. Why don't you come into my library, where we can talk."

As Michael turned to walk back into the apartment, he glimpsed another black-clad figure streaking up the stairs toward them. With one arm, Michael swept Father de Aragon into the apartment. Then he turned, tensed for an attack. The black-clad figure encircled him in a vice-like grip. As he recognized the familiar hold, the rush of adrenalin gave way to surprise and delight. "Father James!"

Father James Talman laughed. "You're old and out of shape. I was in your full view the whole time. Can you imagine what would have happened if I snuck up on you from behind?"

Father James Talman had taught him martial arts. Michael grinned and faced his old friend. Then his grin faded.

Though two decades older than Michael, James always had a boyish face and kept himself in extraordinary physical condition. But almost two years had passed since he was in Rome, and Michael found the change in him disturbing. Beneath the black cassock he still appeared fit, his muscles taut and toned. His face, in stark contrast, bore deeply etched lines of character and care. He looked as if he'd aged twenty years.

"What are you doing in Rome?" Michael asked. "You didn't call."

James's expression hardened. He nodded toward Father de Aragon. "The Society called me back for an emergency meeting," he said tersely. "We're gearing up for a political earthquake in the Vatican. That's why we're here."

Michael thought of the dead priest, Father Pintozzi. "Come inside where we can talk."

He led them down the hallway, through the living area where he normally received guests and into his library. This was the room where Michael liked to do his planning and decision-making, where he felt most at ease. It seemed natural to receive these particular guests in his private retreat.

Father de Aragon paused at the entrance. Michael tried to see it through his eyes. The cavernous room's floor-to-ceiling, custom-made shelves groaned with books in Italian and English. Two sections were reserved for rare and old first editions, and textbooks on international finance and economic theories.

On the far side of the room was a large desk made of dark cherry wood. A storage unit behind it housed current business magazines. The desk was partially covered with papers, a copy of the most recent editions of *Euromoney* and *Institutional Investor*, and a laptop. Next to the computer was a custom-made niche for remote hard drives for back-ups and slots for thumb drives. A multi-landline phone sat on the right side of the desk.

A smaller work unit nearby supported another laptop and a tablet, as well as wireless printers. Four screens were positioned so that when Michael sat at the main desk, he could glance at the data on them as if they were one unit. Two of the screens were split into multiple windows displaying financial information: currency rates, bond rates, commodity prices and stock quotes from around the globe.

They moved to a sitting area away from the desk, next to a mahogany coffee table. Michael motioned them to sit.

"May we speak in English?" Father de Aragon asked in Italian.

"Yes," Michael replied in perfect English. "My mother was Italian-American, and I completed my higher education in the U.S. James and I met when I studied in Georgetown."

"Thank you." Father de Aragon looked Michael in the eyes. "Spanish is my first language, and English is my second. I'm afraid I have not had the time to perfect my Italian."

Michael offered them coffee, which they accepted. "I could use some caffeine just now,"

Father de Aragon said. "I've had a long and difficult journey."

Michael was burning with questions, but he restrained himself while he saw to the comfort of his guests. He pulled out three cups, a sugar bowl and creamer from the coffee service, an heirloom set of creamy porcelain inlaid with delicate swirls of 22-karat gold. The Viscontes had used these demitasse cups for more than two hundred and fifty years. The coffee he poured into a silver samovar, brought back from the Middle East by an ancestor two centuries earlier. As he worked, he reflected on his unexpected company. Yesterday he couldn't get a priest to give him the time of day, and now, two Jesuits showed up on his doorstep.

He couldn't get over the change in James. Since they left college, James had grown more remote and somewhat odd, though in a good way. Their friendship was constantly evolving and increasingly complex. But this change felt different, and profound. Then there was the cassock. The last time Michael remembered seeing James wear one outside of Mass was years ago. He had a feeling too that James deferred to the older priest. And what did their appearance have to do with a political earthquake in the Vatican?

When Michael returned to the library holding the coffee tray, the air seemed warmer compared to the air-conditioning he had blasted into the rest of the apartment. No, that wasn't accurate.

The area around Father de Aragon seemed warmer. It felt soothing, comforting.

He served the coffee, then settled back in his chair. James's eyes indicated Michael should address the older priest.

"You mentioned that you had a long journey, Father de Aragon."

The priest nodded. "I just returned from a mission to South America. More a pleasure trip than anything else. Among other things, I attended a reception in Chile at Aldo Angelini's mountain estate. He threw a party in honor of his grandson's engagement to a young woman from the Romito family of Argentina. Raul Campos, who was attending the celebration, was kind enough to fly me to Santiago to get a commercial flight after I was called back to the Vatican."

Michael put down his coffee cup. He didn't need a Ph.D. in International Finance to recognize the names. In a few short sentences, Father de Aragon had told Michael just how well connected he was. The Angelinis, Camposes and Romitos were three of the most famous families in South America. Between them, they controlled the dollar equivalent of more than $12 billion, and they had influence over much more.

He thought over what he knew of them as he and the priests sipped coffee in silence. The Campos family owned a large paper company in Chile. They also owned Banco Campos, one of Chile's largest banks. It was a source of capital for the rest of Latin America, especially Argentina.

The family had a reputation as astute and honest, but they were opportunists. People who did business with them usually felt a lot poorer, while the Camposes ended up a lot richer. They had no scruples about taking advantage of timidity, naiveté or temporary cash flow problems, and they always seemed to know who suffered from these weaknesses.

The Romito family claimed wealth in the hundreds of millions, which meant they were poor by Campos family standards. Business analysts estimated the Romitos' actual worth at more than $3 billion, and widely believed the lesser claim was a tax dodge. The family built their empire around the Romito Group, a conglomerate of steel mills, oil exploration and construction companies, and railroads. Michael knew they remained citizens of Italy; the family patriarch, Agostino Romito, had served as Mussolini's industry minister before moving to Argentina in 1945. Like the Camposes, the Romitos had a reputation for honesty combined with uncanny business acumen.

Business analysts had puzzled for decades over how Agostino Romito managed to get the capital he needed to found his Argentine empire. Money transfers from Italy were closely monitored after the war, and highly placed people in Italy made it their business to see that Agostino Romito's wealth stayed there.

Nevertheless, Romito's assets mysteriously disappeared from Italy and reappeared in Argentina. Rumors hinted that Agostino Romito had unimpeachable and untouchable help from the Catholic Church, specifically the Jesuits. Father de Aragon's comment recalled those claims, and Michael wondered if they had anything to do with his guests' presence in his study.

Like the Romitos, the Angelini family founded its empire when Aldo and his late father emigrated from Italy after World War II. The family owned a third of Copec, Chile's petroleum conglomerate, as well as a construction business and paint factory. They also made their money magically disappear from Italy and reappear in Chile when they most needed it. They, too, were astute businessmen and great believers in a good education, a Jesuit education.

In Latin America, the Jesuit influence was extremely powerful. Jesuits had baptized, educated, married and buried almost every person of influence there over the last four centuries. Respected for their political astuteness, their connections, and their influence, the Jesuits possessed a trove of information about Latin America's internal political affairs. Influential Latin Americans had a Jesuit confessor, if they had a confessor at all. But every leading family had a Jesuit consigliere.

Michael sipped more coffee. Jesuits, Latin American billionaires, and James's hints of "a political earthquake" in the Vatican. And just possibly a dead Jesuit priest with his throat cut. "I've heard those names before," he said.

"I'm not surprised. You have a doctorate from the University of Rochester in International Finance, correct?" Father de Aragon's question sounded more like a statement.

Michael's unease rose. "You have me at a disadvantage, Father. You seem to know everything about me."

"I did my own research. If you'll allow me, I'll show you." Father de Aragon stood, indicating Michael should follow him. He walked over to Michael's desk. "May I use your computer?" He eyed the equipment critically. "Your system's overdue for an upgrade."

Michael frowned. As a computer fraud expert for the Specialists, he knew his personal system was only a hair's breadth away from state-of-the-art, and he resented hearing a comment on his expertise from a priest.

Father de Aragon booted up the computer and asked Michael to log on under his own password. After Michael complied, the priest typed quickly using only his index fingers. Lines of text appeared on the computer screen.

For the first time, Michael noticed Father de Aragon's hands. The priest was missing the last two fingers of his right hand and the last finger of his left. The remaining fingers functioned normally, but they were mangled, as if healed after an accident in which they were crushed.

Michael glanced up at the priest's face and noticed scar tissue on the left side of his neck, just above his collar. Red and lumpy, it resembled a healed burn.

Father de Aragon typed in a series of access codes. Michael was surprised at the speed with which the priest manipulated them. "We have many levels of protection, and we employ a few codes and tricks to foil potential hackers," de Aragon said.

Educated at Jesuit schools, Michael fully appreciated the intelligence and worldliness of the priests in the Jesuit community. Even so, he was impressed.

"Now you can review our reports on you." Father de Aragon stepped aside so Michael could view the screen.

"Reports? More than one?" Michael frowned as he pressed buttons and scrolled through the displays. He read screen after screen in stunned silence.

Candidate Summary. Press <F1> for full report
Michael Roberto Visconte. Catholic. b. Aug. 2, 1977 1:30 a.m. Son of Lenore Ferruzi (American branch, d.2005 breast cancer) and Giovanni Visconte (Italian branch, d. 2006 coronary disease).

Estd. net worth as of 2006: $142 million.

Attended the Italian-American diplomatic school, and Loyola Academy in Rome. Fordham undergraduate in business, 3.9/4.0, graduated 1997. Masters in Foreign Studies from Georgetown, 1998. Ph.D. in international business and finance, University of Rochester 2001.

Married to Helena Barone (Italian branch), civil ceremony only. May 26, 2005. Two children: Anthony, b. March 18, 2007, now attending St. Bartolome's grade school in Rome, and Luke, b. April 21, 2009.

Recruited for the special branch of the Italian secret service while attending University of Rochester. Cross-border financial crime and cybercrime expert. Currently active. No Society contact as of 2011.

Press <F1> for Full Report
Press <F2> for Family History
Press <F3> for Dun and Bradstreet Report
Press <F4> for Medical History
Press <F5> for Psychological Profile
Press <F6> for Another Search

The Jesuits' summary contained information even his family didn't know. His mother had kept her breast cancer a secret, and his father had told him the true nature of her illness only after she died. The fact that he and Helena hadn't been married in the Church was likewise something they'd kept to themselves. His recruitment information was classified, and yet there it was staring at him from his computer screen.

"This is amazing," Michael said. "You have my entire family tree as far back as the year 1400." He continued scrolling.

It troubled him that the Jesuits had such a precise picture of his finances. But how? Michael never told anyone about his investments. He consistently beat market averages, although the global investment market was a zero-sum game. If Michael outperformed the market average, that meant someone else had to underperform.

He had anticipated the ongoing global financial crisis that first became apparent to most people in September 2008. The U.S. Fed poured hundreds of billions of dollars into its financial system and provided over ten trillion dollars of support and guarantees. As a result of the subsidy to banks' borrowing costs, investors earned close to nothing on "safe" U.S. treasuries. Despite the conditions, Michael had parlayed an inheritance of $62 million into $142 million in under five years, averaging just over eighteen percent per year in hedged returns.

But how did the Jesuits know his net worth?

He paged through the file, stopped among pages of trade details and frowned. "You're keeping better track of my finances than I am. How did you get this information?"

"You'd be surprised how much is publicly available," Father de Aragon said. "Credit reports, bank balances, property records, criminal records, spending habits, health records, leisure activities and romantic habits, they're all easy to find."

"But my trade details aren't, and my computer is virtually unhackable."

"Every computer can be hacked, but don't be concerned. We didn't do that. We used other ways."

Michael shot Father de Aragon a hard look. The only other possibility was that the Jesuits were hacking the computers of the financial institutions with which he traded. He decided to let it go for the moment. He would challenge the priest on other aspects of the data that he found equally unsettling.

"Medical records are privileged. Where did this psychological profile come from?" Michael scanned the screen and turned to Father James, whom he knew was a psychiatrist. "James, did you evaluate me without my permission?"

"It was for the Society's use only," James said without apology.

Michael stared at one priest, then the other. "You seem to have an answer for everything."

"Michael," James said evenly, "as a personal favor, I'm asking you to bear with us and listen with an open mind."

Michael flipped to his high school and college records. He had an IQ of 145 on a Wechsler scale, putting him in the top one percent of the population. He knew some Jesuits had even higher IQs. A few belonged to the Giga Society, which required IQ scores of 196 on specialized tests. Then Michael saw something that made him stop. "Our professors were taking notes on us?"

Father de Aragon nodded. "When the Jesuits identify promising young people, we keep track of them. Jesuit teachers usually write something about the individual, their impressions, their evaluation of the person's strengths and weaknesses."

Michael eyed the text on the screen: a letter of recommendation written by his favorite college professor, Father Conklin, who had died about ten years ago. He read a portion of it:

"In all of my dealings with Michael Visconte, I have found him to be a bright, creative and perceptive individual. He has uncommon self-possession, maturity and consideration for others, rare in one so young. He wears the mantle of his old noble family name well. I recommend him for further Society contact wholeheartedly and without reservation."

Michael had always admired and respected Father Conklin. He remembered the priest's sparkling intellect and simple human decency. He had no idea Father Conklin knew him as anything other than the third-row student who happened to get an A in his class. This letter meant more to Michael than the A ever did.

The report included comments from each of his other Jesuit professors in high school and college as well, dozens of them. After quickly scrolling through, Michael looked up. "This information. Does it come from Church files?"

Neither of the priests answered him.

Michael rephrased his question. "Does it come from a Jesuit database?"

"A proprietary Jesuit database," Father de Aragon said.

There was nothing more to the report—mercifully, Michael thought. They returned to their chairs, and Michael poured them all more coffee. He couldn't help eying Father de Aragon's mangled hands as he handed him his cup.

Father de Aragon followed his glance, and spread his free hand deprecatingly. "They don't look like much, but they get the job done." He paused. "I acquired those scars about thirty years ago in Chile. I was tortured."

He paused, as if to let this sink in. He took a sip of coffee with a smooth and graceful motion, and continued: "I was very lucky. The plastic surgeons were able to reconstruct and save most of the function of my hands. The thumb and first two fingers are especially important to me; I can still hold the host to properly say the Mass."

"I thought clergy were immune to arrest," Michael said.

"Publicly, yes. But much happens in Latin America that isn't publicized. Torture for presumed spies, for instance."

"Were you a spy?" Michael asked.

"Technically, no. I was merely a courier."

"For whom?" Michael's curiosity was fully aroused.

"For the Society, of course," Father de Aragon replied with a slight smile.

This frank admission of espionage puzzled Michael. Over several centuries, the Jesuits had been accused of spying by a variety of governments. Jesuits had been tortured and executed, but had always denied any involvement. Even in the Jesuit academies Michael attended, reports of spying were discredited as the self-serving accusations of paranoid authorities.

"Father, if you were convicted of spying in Chile, you're lucky to be alive."

"I was never convicted of anything."

"Then you didn't talk?"

"On the contrary." Father de Aragon looked down at his deformed hands. "I told them everything. Their torture techniques could make anyone talk." He let out a deep sigh. "My hands were the least of it."

"Then why—"

"I told them everything," the priest continued. "But they couldn't make sense of the information. I didn't know what it meant myself. I was only the courier. The information was in code, an unbreakable code, a Jesuit code."

CHAPTER V

Rome
Sunday, June 16

Michael looked at James in surprise. He had studied codes as part of his training for the Specialists. Most codes were mathematical, or a combination of math and words, often with a code book as a reference key. Some codes posed an enormous challenge, but breaking any code was just a matter of time, intelligence and patience. The closest thing to an unbreakable code used a onetime pad as a key, which had to be delivered to everyone who needed it, and it could only be used once. Even that could be cracked if the pad was intercepted.

"Father, I'm sure the code was ingenious and your captors couldn't figure out how to break it. But there's no such thing as an unbreakable code."

Father de Aragon gave a deep, throaty laugh. "You should have spent more time in our libraries. We have an unfortunate habit of underestimating our ancestors."

Michael remembered the huge libraries filled with accounts of the Jesuits and the learning they had picked up from other cultures throughout the world. Centuries' worth of information written by history's most famous intellectuals. Part of the wealth of the Jesuit community was this vast collection of ancient books, meticulously catalogued and cross referenced.

Michael had assumed the works were pedantic religious texts, irrelevant for his study of international business, and later, international crime. Apparently, he had missed something important.

Father de Aragon explained. "We first got the idea in the sixteenth century from Matteo Ricci, who applied masterful memory techniques to learning Chinese and classical Chinese on his mission to China. The Chinese had great respect for scholars, and Matteo Ricci's feats of memory further endeared him to Governor Lu Wangai in the 1500s. Ricci became a favorite in the Chinese court, but jealous Dominicans and Fransicans successfully petitioned the Vatican to outlaw Ricci's approach of embracing Chinese culture to win converts." Father de Aragon's face darkened when he mentioned the Dominicans and Franciscans.

"Father de Aragon is the Society's foremost scholar in memory science," James added.

Michael was intrigued. "So what were his memory techniques?"

Father de Aragon seemed energized by his interest. "Ricci created memory palaces in his mind. Each item in the palace represented a series of concepts. The rooms and locations within the palace served as directories and files, similar to computer data storage. Ricci instantaneously learned, retained and retrieved hundreds of new Chinese *kanji*, to the astonished delight of Chinese nobles."

"Did he invent that technique?"

"No, but he developed it. Written evidence of mnemonic arts dates as far back as 2,000 B.C., and people likely used memory techniques long before that"

Father de Aragon rose and began pacing as he went on. "Aristotle was convinced that a trained memory helped the development of logical thought processes. Pliny wrote of Roman memory experts in his *Historia Naturalis*. Cicero praised memory training in his *De Oratore*. In *Ad Herennium*, another Cicero text, he discussed several memory devices employed in his time. Quintilian wrote a handbook on oratory, in which he explained his own memory devices. He believed that a trained memory was essential for an accomplished orator. St. Thomas Aquinas, born in 1225 A.D., a year after the death of Francis of Assisi, used memory arts in the study of philosophy and theology. Francesco Panigarola, born a couple of decades before Matteo Ricci, could recall hundreds of thousands of ideas at will, and he documented his memory techniques."

"Why is this so important to the Jesuit community? And what does it have to do with why you're here?" The lecture was fascinating, and any other time Michael would have enjoyed it, but he couldn't forget what James had said earlier...or the events of yesterday morning.

Father de Aragon answered the first question, but sidestepped the second. "When St. Ignatius of Loyola founded the Society of Jesus in 1540, he was an avid student of memory arts. Matteo Ricci studied to become a priest in the late 1500s, and memory training was a required part of the curriculum at the Jesuit college in Rome. After Ricci, we explored and expanded the limits of the mind for more than four hundred years. We traveled and learned control of mind and body from the fakirs of India, control techniques of the Buddhists in China and Japan, the spiritual arts of shamans in Africa, trance states of Indian medicine men in North and South America, the magic of the Mayan shamans, hypnosis, extra-sensory techniques and telepathy. Year after year we improve, free of the nagging responsibilities of earning a living, raising a family, caring for aged relatives or shepherding a community of the faithful. We are always expanding the collective consciousness of the Society."

Michael laughed. "'We are the Borg. Resistance is futile.'"

Father de Aragon glanced down at him with a friendly smile. "Yes, I see how it could sound funny, at first. But it is a serious business. Language is an example of a combination of memory techniques and codes, but at a largely unconscious level. We're a symbolic species.

Symbols are the heart of all human communication."

Michael nodded. "We encode a sound to an object or meaning."

"Yes, and more. We encode feelings. Sometimes even against our will. The name of an enemy, for instance, can cause a change of feeling or state within a person, even when one doesn't want it to."

"I've had that experience," Michael said dryly.

Father de Aragon smiled. "Of course, it works the same for positive feelings. Formal memory training consciously employs techniques our brain naturally uses on an unconscious level."

"How does it work?"

"Picture in your mind ten pretty virgin girls sitting on chairs reading the Bible," Father de Aragon said.

Michael smiled. "Got it."

"Now think of this sentence: 'Pretty Virgins Never Read Trash.'".

"Okay."

"Tell me the first letters of each word in the sentence."

"PVNRT," Michael responded.

"Right," Father de Aragon said. "You may remember from high school chemistry: $PV = nRT$, the equation for the gaseous equilibrium of pressure, volume, and temperature where n is the molar value and R is a constant."

Michael grinned. "Yes, but it's much easier to remember your way."

"Now let's get more complicated. I'm going to match numbers with phonetic sounds. Double letters don't count. For instance, 0 is an 's' or a 'z' sound; 1 is a 'd' or 't' sound; 2 is an 'n' sound; 3 is an 'm' sound; 4 is an 'r' sound; 5 is an 'l' sound; 6 is a 'ch' or 'sh' sound; 7 is a hard 'g', hard 'c' or a 'k' sound; 8 is a 'v' or an 'f' sound, and 9 is a 'b' or 'p' sound."

Father de Aragon paused to let Michael get the gist of what he was saying. Then he spoke rapidly: "It is much easier to remember the sentence, 'Michael Visconte makes excellent coffee,' than the string of numbers the sentence represents: '375807213707052178'."

He slowed his speech and continued. "It's a code. Once one knows the code, it is simple to create words to match numbers. Words are easier to remember than numbers. Then one can make mental pictures out of the words. Pictures are easier to remember than words."

"You make it seem easy," Michael said.

"The Jesuits have developed hundreds of memory techniques."

"So what does this have to do with creating an unbreakable code? Any code that incorporated these techniques could be broken."

Father de Aragon nodded. "You are correct, provided one can establish the frame of reference. Without that, one cannot break the code."

"I don't understand," Michael said.

"During World War II, the Americans used the Navajo Indian language to transmit messages. It was a clever idea and a successful ploy for a very long time. The transmissions were frequently intercepted, but the other side couldn't crack the code. No frame of reference. The Axis powers didn't know the transmissions were a language until a linguist figured it out."

"But they eventually cracked the code."

"That is the problem with using a language, however arcane," Father de Aragon agreed. "Even the language of a dead civilization can be deciphered if there is enough information to establish the frame of reference. Hieroglyphics is an example."

"Latin is another," Michael said.

Father de Aragon let out another deep throaty laugh. "Latin is still young and alive for Jesuits."

"But how can you make an unbreakable code without a frame of reference?"

"You can't really," Father de Aragon admitted. "You can, however, limit the number of people who know the frame of reference."

"By using code books."

Father de Aragon shook his head. "Very messy. Code books can be copied or found. And they are damning evidence."

"You're telling me the Jesuits have a code without code books?"

"I'm telling you that the Jesuits have many such codes."

Michael stared at de Aragon in amazement.

"Code study is voluntary, of course," the priest said. "Soon after ordination, three compatible Jesuits work together for five years developing their own secret code. They eat, sleep and think together, combining their common experiences, their knowledge of Greek, Latin, math, private childhood experiences, parts of the Mass, memory arts and whatever else they want to throw into the mix."

Father de Aragon paused again to let the implication of that sink in.

Their coffee had long since gone cold, and Michael reached over and snuffed the flame underneath the samovar. The coffee in it must have the consistency of mud. "Why three people?" he asked. "Doesn't the risk of a leak increase exponentially, by the square of the number of people who have access to the information?"

Father de Aragon gave Michael a slight nod. "Impressive observation. We accept that risk. The investment of time and energy is enormous. When a code master dies, or is inaccessible, the third priest is a backup."

"Then why not use more than three?"

A pained expression flashed across Father de Aragon's face, and he glanced at Father James. For a moment he seemed to retreat into his own thoughts. Then he spoke again. "We are, after all, only human. It is better to limit the number of code masters in each group. When two of the priests in a group are gone, the code dies with them, and it is up to the remaining groups of code masters to pass information."

"You were carrying a memorized coded message that you couldn't break," Michael said with dawning awareness. "Your Chilean government captors had no proof, no code books, even though you were cooperating."

Father de Aragon nodded, in the manner of a proud teacher. "Eventually, the Society found me and used their influence to free me." He paused, then smiled slightly. "My reception in Chile has improved since then."

His voice was compelling, almost hypnotic. Michael felt as if the sound was carrying him along. He wasn't in charge of the conversation, he realized. The priest was revealing things in the order he wanted them revealed.

"You sought me out," Michael said. "Why? Why show me and tell me everything you have so far? What do you want from me?"

"The Society needs a favor," Father de Aragon answered. "Do you recall Father Mark Manion?"

Michael frowned. "He was beaten. A Vigilo found him. Then Father Manion disappeared." Two weeks ago, give or take a day, if Michael remembered correctly.

"He was bludgeoned to death in the Vatican," Father James said. "We found his mutilated body in the catacombs under St. Peter's."

CHAPTER VI

Rome
Sunday, June 16

Michael sat motionless, staring across the coffee table at the two Jesuits. Father Mark Manion. He remembered the incident too well. Two weeks earlier, a priest in his early sixties stumbled out of the Vatican into the arms of Lorenzo Colonna, a startled rookie Vigilo. Blood had run down one side of the priest's face and matted in his hair. He was incoherent and disoriented.

When Michael later questioned the frightened Vigilo, Colonna explained he didn't know what to do. The priest's injuries looked grave, and the man's greyish pallor and unintelligible muttering horrified him. "I propped him up, and he vomited," Colonna had said. "Almost hit some bystanders. If it weren't for his cassock, I'd have thought he was an addict who'd just been roughed up. Then two more priests showed up and led him back onto Vatican soil. They said they would take care of things. I was relieved. Who wouldn't be?"

Colonna couldn't tell Michael the order to which the priests belonged or even if all three belonged to the same one. It happened so fast, and the priests seemed to know what they were doing. Not that Colonna ever would have thought to question a priest's judgment.

Later, when he got off duty, he grew worried about the injured man. He made inquiries as to how the priest was faring, but the Vatican denied knowledge of the incident. He walked around the Vatican, looking for the two priests who had come to the other one's rescue, but now every priest he saw looked alike. In his confusion, he hadn't taken a good look at their faces.

Colonna at least had the presence of mind to file a report. A member of the Polizia, who wanted no trouble with the Vatican, referred the matter to the Carabinieri. They handed it on to the Specialists since, among other things, the Specialists were rumored to be involved in an investigation that had something to do with priests and the Vatican.

Michael's own inquiries turned up a name, Father Mark Manion, but nothing more. Michael's staff checked Rome's hospitals. A priest had broken a foot and another fell off a bicycle and injured a shoulder, but no priest was brought in with head injuries. They checked hospitals on the outskirts of Rome, but nothing turned up there either. Private doctors known to treat injuries on the quiet were close-mouthed, and neighbors near their clinics didn't remember seeing an injured man being brought in for aid that day.

Michael's further inquiries in the Vatican were met with either polite stonewalling or assertive denial. Now he knew why.

***

"Let me guess," Michael said slowly. "Father Manion's genitals were cut off and found in his mouth."

He waited for a reaction, but Father de Aragon didn't flinch. The priest must know the details of Father Pintozzi's death. In fact, he seemed to take it for granted that Michael would fill in the blanks; de Aragon seemed to know what was in his mind. Michael felt a renewed respect for the man, and he also knew it would be very dangerous to underestimate him.

"Why didn't you go to the Roman police?" Michael asked.

"This has nothing to do with Rome. I chose you because Father James trusts you. That means everything in the Jesuit community," Father de Aragon said. "And because…"

"Because you knew Father Manion. He was a member of your code group." Another guess, but Michael felt confident of it. Father Manion was the right age, and Father de Aragon seemed to have a personal interest in the case.

"No, he wasn't." Father de Aragon said. "I believe you met Father Graf in the Vatican

Museum yesterday. He is in my code group. Soon you will meet the third member, Father Pleurre. Father Manion was merely a good friend. I chose you because you found the body of Father Matteo Pintozzi." Father de Aragon paused, then said the last thing Michael would have expected. "My friend...and former lover."

Michael's stomach knotted in revulsion. Father de Aragon had seemed like the perfect priest—poised and calm, with the dignity that comes from years of self-respect and self-knowledge. He had not pegged the man as a homosexual. He felt a stab of betrayal. He glanced at Father James, but James's face was neutral.

Michael looked back at Father de Aragon. The priest's expression held no apology. He looked serene, as if he had never experienced fear or pain. His face was that of a saint.

Quietly, Father de Aragon answered the question Michael had not asked. "It was just after Father Matteo moved to the Vatican. Everyone liked Matteo. He was vibrant and seductive, full of life and ambition. He was blessed with a quick mind and uncommon physical beauty. We had an affair for about a year. He initiated it. I broke it off about five years ago to renew my vows of celibacy."

"What do you mean, you renewed your vows?"

"I had been celibate since ordination. I knew I was a homosexual when I joined the Society, but that isn't why I became a priest."

"What do you mean by that?" Michael's voice held a trace of accusation.

"When I was ordained," Father de Aragon said, "many homosexuals became priests because it was one of the few places to run. In the mid-sixties, when I took my vows, homosexuals were vilified by society."

"I'm not sure things are much different today, especially in Italy," Michael said. "But you're a priest. Priests are supposed to be celibate." He gave James a questioning look. This time James nodded. Michael felt a surge of relief. At least one icon had not been destroyed.

"Yes," Father de Aragon said, without apology. "But Matteo never took the vow of chastity seriously. The priesthood, and the access it gave him to other young adult men, was his private candy store. He was an ambitious opportunist. I am highly placed in the Society. Matteo thought I could help him."

"Did you?"

"Yes. But only because it was good for the Society. He became the Jesuits' most talented hedge fund manager. I recommended him, because he had the best qualifications. Investments were his passion. He had a gambler's appetite for risk, and a mathematician's talent for managing it. As a money manager, he knew how to get the optimum profit out of any market betting opportunity. He was also the most talented Jesuit in the memory arts."

Hedge fund manager, Michael thought. Money provided a powerful motive for murder. A hedge fund manager was not an ordinary money manager. Hedge funds were private and catered to wealthy individuals with a net worth of at least one million dollars or an annual income of more than two hundred thousand dollars. Some hedge funds had even higher requirements, demanding a minimum investment of ten million dollars or more. Some hedge funds only allowed banks, insurance companies or other financial institutions to invest with them. It was an elite and secretive community that skated back and forth across the line of insider trading. Mutual funds had to publicly report their performance figures, but hedge funds weren't required to report their track record.

Michael managed his personal wealth as if it were a hedge fund. Hedge funds used high-risk sophisticated financial techniques, such as borrowing money and borrowing and selling securities one didn't own, hoping to buy them back later at a lower price and make extraordinary capital gains. That was the likely reason for Father de Aragon's visit to the wealthy South Americans. They were investors. Michael would get back to that later, but for now he said, "So you remained friends with Father Pintozzi."

The priest nodded. "But not close friends. Matteo wanted a higher position in the Society. James did a psychological evaluation on him a few years ago, and found him unsuited for advancement. I think Matteo felt I blocked him."

Michael shook his head. "I can see there's a lot I don't know about the Jesuits."

"Especially about St. Ignatius," Father de Aragon said with a slight smile.

"What do you mean?"

"You and I share a common ancestor." Father de Aragon paused to let Michael absorb this. "Our ancestor aided St. Ignatius when he made his pilgrimage to Jerusalem."

Michael frowned. "None of my ancestors lived in Spain."

"This ancestor moved from Spain to Paliano after her marriage. In 1524, St. Ignatius passed through Paliano, where he received financial assistance from Giovanna de Aragon, the wife of Asconio Visconte. Giovanna was your great-grandmother several times removed and the sister of one of mine. That makes us distant cousins."

Michael knew his ancestors had moved from Paliano to Rome, but he had never heard of Giovanna de Aragon. He would check the old family Bibles when he had a chance. Even as he thought it, Michael knew it was unnecessary; everything the priest said would prove accurate.

He turned the conversation back toward things he understood. "You said Father Pintozzi managed a hedge fund. How was he doing?"

"We just did a thorough audit. His fund was up more than 24 percent, and the year is barely half over. For the past six years, his fund has been up more than 38 percent annually."

"Is that 38 percent after fees?"

"Yes."

Michael was stunned. That kind of consistent performance was impossible without cheating. He was about to point that out, but thought better of it. "What are the fees?"

Father de Aragon grinned. "We charge eight percent per year plus 30 percent of the upside."

The fees were the highest in the money management industry. "Citadel, one of the most successful hedge funds in the world, only charges about six percent per year," Michael said.

"Yes, but they don't come close to matching our success, do they?"

In fact, no one came close to matching those numbers. Not even Warren Buffett during the period of his original partnership, from 1956 to when he closed it down in 1969. He had achieved a compound annual growth rate of 31 percent, but his fees were negligible. Yet the Jesuits claimed their hedge fund returned 38 percent net of fees.

Michael regarded Father de Aragon with skepticism. The priest wasn't asking him to believe this was a freakish run of luck. To achieve those kinds of returns, the Jesuits either did something illegal or they were lying.

Father de Aragon ignored Michael's expression and continued. "Matteo was a financial genius, and he put his genius to work in the marketplace. He had an uncanny ability to see clean and elegant solutions to complex financial problems."

Michael shook his head. "It sounds like a Ponzi scheme."

Father de Aragon chuckled. "No, it's not. We'll explain more another time."

"Then, as one cousin to another, who killed Father Pintozzi and why?" Michael was confused. If the fund had performed poorly or if fraud was involved, there would be a motive, but who wanted to kill a golden goose?

Father de Aragon hesitated, all trace of levity gone. "I can't be sure."

"How did Father Pintozzi invest the money?"

James interrupted. "Come to the Jesuit quarters in the Vatican on Monday afternoon at three. We'll introduce you to special members of the Society, and many of your questions will be answered then."

"Wait. Why are you coming to me now? And how does any of this tie in to what you said before, about a political earthquake at the Vatican?"

Father de Aragon locked eyes with him. "We're asking for your help, the way St. Ignatius asked Giovanna of Aragon so many centuries ago."

***

After Michael finally closed the door on the priests, he became aware of an urgent need to urinate, and he was ravenously hungry and thirsty. Now that he thought about it, the two Jesuits hadn't asked for the use of Michael's bathroom or for something to eat.

The apartment was cold from the air-conditioning, as if it had blasted all day. Michael turned it off and put on a sweater. When he went back into the library to collect the coffee tray, he noticed that the room felt comfortable. So much so that he prepared some food for himself and ate there. A casual glance at his watch as he finished shocked him; it was 4 p.m. The Jesuit priests had arrived around 9 in the morning. The whole day had passed, yet Michael would have sworn they had talked for less than two hours.

His feelings about that talk were mixed. He admired and respected the Jesuits, and he owed them a debt. Jesuit guidance had once helped him out of a suicidal depression. But scars of deep personal grief colored his view of the Church, and of the Jesuits as part of it.

Half longing and half fearful, Michael gave himself up to memory. He'd graduated from college early. He was a gifted student on an accelerated program. At Fordham, Michael fell in love with a young Italian girl, Irena Scarpa. Her father made and repaired custom shoes, earning a meager but honest living. His parents initially resisted the match, but they relented when they realized that Michael was desperately in love. He even considered dropping out of Fordham after his freshman year so he could stay permanently in Rome and marry Irena.

The summer of his sophomore year changed everything. When Michael returned to the United States for the fall term, Irena was pregnant and too ashamed to tell him. She was afraid he would think she was manipulating him into marriage, and that his wealthy and well-born parents would think so too. So she kept silent.

Unable to get a legal abortion in Catholic Italy, she went to a back-alley quack. She got her abortion and along with it, a perforated uterus. Too frightened and ashamed to ask for help, Irena went home to her room. She lost quarts of blood before her mother found her and took her to the hospital. Thirty-six hours after her abortion, Irena died from shock and massive blood loss.

Part of Michael died with her. He blamed Church influence for the Italian law that made it nearly impossible for Irena to buy birth control pills or him to buy condoms, and for the absence of decent abortion clinics.

Most of all, he blamed himself for being careless enough to put her in jeopardy, and for not bringing contraception from the United States. He also blamed himself for not trying to draw her out, for not making her tell him everything on her mind. For not marrying her when he had the chance.

His faith provided no comfort. He had never felt so useless and alone. A suffocating darkness clouded his thoughts: the end of living and the beginning of mere survival. Only the counseling of a few concerned Jesuits pulled him out of a suicidal tailspin.

After Irena's death Michael threw himself into his studies. He worked out every day with a rigorous exercise program, the only affirmation of life he allowed himself. His good looks and courtly manner earned him friends and popularity, but he never felt close to anyone. Especially to any woman.

He left Italy and went for his masters at Georgetown, then went on to the University of Rochester for his Ph.D. He knew he could drown another few years in study, completely occupying his mind so that painful thoughts could not find their way to the surface.

When the Specialists recruited Michael, he saw it as a way to do something useful with his life. The Specialists promised to make positive changes in Italian society, and they needed bright, energetic men like him. For a few years it was perfect. The Specialists fulfilled their promise, and Michael felt he had a purpose again. He rose to the top of the ranks in Rome.

Throughout the late 1970s and early 1980s, Italy was plagued with terrorist bombings and kidnappings. After the Red Brigade assassinated former Prime Minister Aldo Moro in 1978, the Specialists were granted the authority they needed to turn the tide of the war against terrorism. By the late 1990s Italy's streets, train stations, and airports were safe once more.

When Michael met Helena, he was still hiding in his work. He had dated a lot of women after Irena, but he quickly grew tired of them, or they grew tired of his distance. Helena was different. Her lively, outgoing manner and her ability to see beauty everywhere attracted him. He enjoyed her company and missed her when they weren't together.

They dated for a few months, and to his surprise, Michael asked Helena to marry him. He told her about Irena and his difficulty feeling attachment to a woman. Headstrong and determined, Helena agreed to marry him, but made him promise to commit one hundred percent, and said she would hold him to it.

She'd wanted a church ceremony, but Michael couldn't face it, even when Father James offered to perform it. His loss of faith and his loss of love were inextricably intertwined. They had a simple civil ceremony instead. Now his job was threatening the security of his family, something Michael had promised would never happen. He always held something back from Helena; he'd welshed on the deal, and despised himself for it.

He sometimes wondered about the child he and Irena would have had when he looked at his sons, Luke and Anthony. He tried not to brood, but lately he found buried memories of Irena rising to the surface every day along with his feelings of longing and guilt. He pushed them back, but they always resurfaced. He didn't know why, but during the past few weeks he couldn't turn his thoughts away from Irena's memory.

Helena never complained, but he knew it lurked below the surface. Sooner or later, she would challenge him. She'd sworn to hold him to his commitment, and Helena always kept her promises.

CHAPTER VII

Ostia
Monday, June 17

The sound of shouts and running feet from the garden below brought Michael out of the bathroom, his shaving half-finished. Bright morning sunlight streamed into the room from the open French doors to the balcony overlooking the garden.

His reflexes took over as he slipped into his pants and a pair of topsiders, then ran out of his room and down the stairs. The door to the garden was open, and there was no one in sight. He rushed onto the patio just in time to see his gardener, Lorenzo, chasing a dark-clad figure. Michael flung himself after them both, and quickly overtook the older man.

"Go back and check on the family," Michael shouted. Lorenzo hesitated, then turned back. He wasn't fit enough to keep up the chase.

In seconds, Michael was on the intruder's heels. The dark-clad man whirled and landed a glancing blow with a hard object on the right side of Michael's head, then turned and kept running. Dazed, Michael continued his pursuit, but his stride was less steady and the man easily gained several yards.

The interloper reached the six-foot garden wall and lunged for the top. Michael grabbed him by his calves and pulled. The man kicked downward, hard and vicious. His shoe grazed Michael's right temple. Michael flinched and ducked, slackening his grip. As the intruder pulled free, Michael spotted a holstered gun under his jacket.

The man scrambled over the wall. Michael ran back toward the gate. It was open. As he rounded the gate posts, he heard tires crunching gravel. A car, presumably carrying the intruder, was speeding off down the road. It was too far away for Michael to see the license plate. Disappointed and angry, his head throbbing, Michael strode back to the house.

Lorenzo ran from the patio to meet him. "You're hurt!"

Michael shrugged. "It's nothing. Did you get a look at him?"

"I'm sorry, *Dottore*." Lorenzo always addressed him using the honorific for those with a Ph.D. "It all happened so fast."

"What happened?"

Lorenzo looked unsure. "Signora Visconte was having breakfast on the terrace, and she saw a man on the other side of the garden taking photographs. He was partly behind the bushes. When I went after him, he ran."

"Too bad."

"Was he a paparazzo? Signora Visconte is a Barone, and people might be interested in reading about the Visconte family."

Michael's mouth turned up slightly. "I wish it were only that. I'm afraid our little family is not of much interest to the press. Besides, a paparazzo wouldn't carry a gun."

Lorenzo's face registered his shock.

They walked into the house, and Michael went to the bathroom. He examined the right side of his head. It was tender from his assailant's kick and earlier blow, probably from the camera, but the man had been off balance and hadn't given the blow much force. His heel had left an abrasion; Michael cleaned it and then splashed cold water on his face. The water made him feel better.

He left the bathroom to find Lorenzo in the hall, hovering and anxious.

"Where are the children?" Michael asked.

"They were playing inside. Signora Visconte went to check on them," Lorenzo replied.

Michael went to find Helena. She was in the playroom with the boys, who were oblivious to the commotion. Anthony and Luke had eaten earlier, and they were contentedly playing video games. If a bomb had gone off in the garden, they wouldn't have noticed.

Helena gave Michael a questioning look, but he shook his head. He kissed her and said good morning to the boys. Helena drew breath to speak, but Michael cut her off. "We'll talk after I check the grounds," he said.

Helena nodded. She looked concerned, even angry, but not panicked. A brave woman, his wife. Suddenly he found himself grateful that she didn't rattle easily.

He headed upstairs to finish shaving. He knew Helena would ask him again to stop his investigations, and he dreaded the conversation.

Shaved and ready to face the day, Michael patrolled the villa. The Visconte family had owned it for three centuries. The incident with the gun-toting photographer worried him; he would ask the local police about any reports of strangers loitering around the area, or delivery men stopping at neighboring houses.

He saw nothing anywhere on the grounds that gave him cause for immediate alarm. But this was Italy. Car bombings, kidnappings and murders were embedded in her recent history. He'd call the office and arrange a security detail as soon as he got back to the villa.

He thought about how lucky he had been so far in his career, and perhaps how foolish. He and Helena lived a relatively open lifestyle here in Ostia; they had no electrified fences, no heavy weapons at their home, no vicious guard dogs. He owned a gun, but kept it locked away where the boys couldn't get at it. Danger to his family caused by his job was an unpleasant fact Michael hadn't wanted to face. He'd been kidding himself, he realized, thinking the villa's relative isolation was enough to keep them safe. Helena hated the security precautions they did take, mostly in Rome, and wasn't shy about telling him so. No wonder she wanted him to leave the Specialists. Today's incident had pointed up the lack of safeguards at the villa, and would be more ammunition for Helena.

He finished his patrol at the garden gate and looked down the winding gravel access road shaded by tall oak trees. Empty, not a car or living creature in sight. He shifted his attention to the gate, hand-wrought iron wedged into the braccio-thick stone of the massive garden walls. A *braccio* was a Renaissance unit of measurement meaning an arm, but it varied. Michael's walls measured about 66 cm, or around 26 inches.

Statues of putti, small Cupid-like angels, sat atop the gateposts. Michael looked up at them. "You aren't doing a good job of keeping out intruders. You're just sitting there." He walked back toward the garden and locked the gate behind him, vowing to arrange more protection for his family within the hour.

As he neared the house, Helena came running towards him. In her cotton summer dress, she looked like a carefree teenager. She held out his cell phone as she reached him. "It's someone from the office for you."

Michael took the phone. "Hello?"

A muffled voice answered in slow, measured tones. "If it was easy to get pictures of your family, Mr. Visconte, just think how easy it would be for us to kill them."

He felt dizzy for a moment as the call ended. Helena, still next to him, threw him an anxious glance. "What is it?"

He managed to keep calm. "It's not important. They're just encouraging me to get back to work. I need to make another call. I'll join you at the house when I'm finished checking out the grounds."

Helena looked skeptical, but kept silent and walked back toward the house. If she'd seen through his explanation—and she likely had, as he'd held no conversation with the stranger on the phone—she'd chosen not to make an issue of it. At least, not yet. Michael called his office and requested two of the Specialists' best men to watch the grounds outside the villa. The arrangements made, he began a closer check of the property.

A statue of an ancient Roman noblewoman, occupying a sheltered niche, seemed to eye Michael as he walked along. It was a statue of Julia, the daughter of Caesar Augustus, sculpted during her lifetime almost two thousand years ago. He passed manicured bushes that lined the garden pathways, scarcely noticing the winding rose trellises and flowerbeds with bright mixtures of summer blossoms. He circled the fountain in the middle of the garden, with its four trumpeting angels spouting water in graceful arcs, and glanced at the pool in the large marble basin. Then he moved on to the boys' play area next to the house.

The play area held swings, slides, a sandbox, and a small wading pool. Michael tested the swings and slides until he was satisfied they hadn't been tampered with. He raked the sandbox, but found nothing. He looked in the wading pool and swished his hand in the water. The pool seemed safe.

He went inside and up to his sons' playroom, with its wall of books, games and a television with a satellite dish and Xbox. Luke and Anthony were mesmerized by their video game—*Grabbed by the Ghoulies*, which both of them found inexplicably fascinating. Luke grabbed it first thing almost every morning. He shooed his two sons outside and then examined the room. Everything seemed as usual.

He walked through the house and went back out to the double tennis court on the other side. He paced the court and checked the net. Nothing.

He looked across the garden, at Helena's small studio where she drew the advertising art she sold and painted the landscapes and seascapes she loved. He hurried over and opened the door. The pungent smell of oil paints made him sneeze. He prowled through the studio, part of his mind noting with admiration her current work, a nearly finished view from one of the seven hills of Rome. The room held no hidden dangers.

He left the studio and lingered outside it, uneasy. He was sure he hadn't missed anything, but that was what dead men always thought. He made the rounds again, but as before, found nothing.

By the time he finally sat down for breakfast, it was 8:30. A maid had cleared away the dishes from earlier and laid out a breakfast for him on the terrace. Helena joined him and had coffee while he ate. He told her about his visit from the two Jesuit priests, and she grew silent. She was putting up a brave front, but the photographer had worried her, and she was more watchful of the children than usual. Michael wondered how she would react if she knew about the telephoned threat. He was glad he hadn't told her.

After breakfast, Michael and Lorenzo patrolled the grounds again, checked the integrity of the walls and rechecked the villa's unused windows and doors. Michael alerted the servants to be on the lookout for anything out of the ordinary in or around the grounds. He hoped it would be enough, especially once the men from the Specialists arrived.

By ten, Michael was ready to leave. As he walked through the garden to the car, he saw his son Anthony watching Lorenzo, concentrating on the gardener's hands as Lorenzo whittled away at a piece of wood to make a flute. The gardener held a Swiss army pocket knife and skillfully shaped the instrument with short, deft strokes.

Anthony held a similar knife and piece of wood, and attempted to duplicate Lorenzo's strokes.

Michael smiled. He had loved carving wood as a boy. Once all this was over, he resolved to spend more time with his sons and teach them these small skills.

Helena had borne most of the responsibility for raising the boys. His sons exhibited good manners and social confidence. Their poise appeared natural, but it didn't come naturally to any child. His sons' social savvy came from Helena's patient coaching. Michael had very little to do with it, and he felt a stab of guilt at the thought.

Helena came up to him as he reached the car. She eyed the abrasion at his temple, then looked him in the eye. "Going to work?"

"Yes." She knew he was. Her question signaled a discussion he didn't want to have right now.

"Don't you think it's time to leave?"

"Helena—"

"It's not just us anymore."

"You knew what I did for a living when you married me."

She seemed to consider that for a long moment. "No," she finally said. "Not really. I knew about *la bustarella,* the little envelope, and how it drives our economy of kickbacks and bribery. I even knew the Mafia murdered their own. But I lived a sheltered life. I never realized violence could touch our family."

He knew it was true. Most people in Italy thought about Mafia murders as isolated incidents that happened to someone else.

Helena continued. "I never thought it could touch the Church. That poor dead man. How could priests get involved with that kind of violence?"

Michael took a deep breath. "It does have the earmarks of a Mafia crime, but something isn't right. This situation is more complex. The Mafia may be involved, but there's more to it than that. Still, crime is crime. It always escalates. And organized crime doesn't start with violence. It starts with money."

"I've never understood that."

"You've always had money," Michael said with a slight smile.

"But surely they have enough."

"It's never enough." They'd had this discussion before, but once he got going it was hard to stop. "If you get involved with money crimes, it isn't enough to be a steady earner. They always want you to produce more. Kick more money up the food chain. So the criminals keep diversifying. They start with extortion, prostitution, gambling, bank robbery, embezzlement. Kidnapping is a way to get more money and intimidate opposition. When that still doesn't bring in enough, they smuggle and deal drugs. Somewhere along the line, they probably got the priests involved in a small way. Then they increase the pressure."

Something nagged at him as he spoke, a subtle thing he hadn't had time to chase down. Mafia involvement, Father Pintozzi's hedge fund returns, his position among the Jesuits... He thought of Roberto Calvi and the Vatican Bank scandal. After Calvi's murder, it was hard to see what would motivate the Vatican to get involved in financial crimes again. There had to be more to Pintozzi's death—and the threat to Michael's own family—than that.

"But murder," Helena said, and shivered. "What is the point?"

He shrugged. "Money. It buys sex and power. There's also revenge, maintaining control, and silencing witnesses."

She gazed thoughtfully at the garden. "But this young priest. How could he be involved? The murderer took such a risk..."

"Yes." That was another thing that bothered Michael. "It was as if he took personal pleasure in killing Father Pintozzi. Or he's a thrill-seeker. Or both." A rare motivation, thrill-killing, and a frightening one. Though this murderer seemed to be a different type of thrill-seeker. His motive may have been revenge or control, but this killing had an element of recklessness, as if its perpetrator believed he couldn't get caught.

"Are you sure *you* aren't a thrill seeker?" Helena said.

Michael looked at her in surprise.

"It's as if your investigations fill a need that we can't," she said. "You need to chase the bad guys. But you have to choose, and I won't give you long to make up your mind. Not when our children's lives are at stake. What is more important to you, the call of the Church or the safety of your family?"

He had no answer for her, except the one she didn't want to hear—that both mattered, and he couldn't choose. He kissed her cheek, then got in the car and drove away.

CHAPTER VIII

Rome
Monday, June 17

Michael drove into Rome down the Appian Way. The wide, cypress-lined road had been built by third-century B.C. slaves to accommodate the breadth of four chariots. The early morning traffic from the seaside had already abated; he made the trip in thirty minutes.

He spent the next hour briefing his department on his lack of progress over the weekend and on the intruder at his house. At his desk, once more reviewing the old reports on the Vatican, he heard a stir outside his office. He looked up to see the stately figure of Father de Aragon in the doorway. Behind the priest, he saw several members of the department staring.

"May I come in?" Father de Aragon sounded as self-assured as ever, his violet eyes glowing with intelligence and good will.

"Of course, Father." Michael waved him inside. "I didn't expect to see you until the meeting this afternoon."

Father de Aragon nodded and shut the office door behind him. He carried a worn black leather briefcase. "I want to give you something before the meeting." The priest opened the briefcase and pulled out a sheaf of yellowed papers. "These are some of Father Mark Manion's private letters to me. Also a few letters from Father James."

Michael couldn't hide his surprise. "Letters. Not e-mail?"

"Some of the letters predate e-mail," Father de Aragon said. "And later, Father Manion grew suspicious of our e-mail system. Father Manion was not in my code group. Neither is James. The letters are in English, and they were hand-delivered by trusted Jesuits. I thought this would help you understand us better before the meeting. I have marked certain passages of particular importance." Sadness crossed his face. He looked down at the papers and hesitated. "I probably shouldn't have kept them." He sighed heavily. "But now I'm glad I did. Keep them as long as you need them, but I want them back eventually. He was my friend and a courageous man."

The thought that crossed his mind then, Michael didn't want to voice. Father de Aragon seemed to guess it. "No," he said with a wry smile. "We weren't lovers. Father Manion was celibate, and heterosexual."

Michael felt ashamed. He glanced down at the letters. When he looked up again, Father de Aragon was smiling: radiant, forgiving, accepting.

"You are too hard on yourself," he said kindly. "I'll go now. I'll see you at the meeting." The priest left the room with regal dignity, leaving Michael alone in his office with the letters.

Michael flipped through the stack, eyeing the dates. They were arranged in chronological order, beginning in 1974 and ending in 1995. Father de Aragon had marked various passages in red. Michael lowered himself into his chair and began reading.

***

Rome, 15 December, 1974
Dear Paolo,

The collapse of Franklin National Bank is the largest bank crash in the history of the United States. Michele Sindona was arrested. Now he's internationally famous for his bold financial crimes as well as his bizarre sex life. He has a wife and several mistresses, but they also say he slept with his grandmother until he was fifteen.

I don't know how true that story is, but it is true that Sindona laundered money for the Sicilian Mafia, and he had links to the U.S. Mafia as well. I managed to get a look at a report from the U.S. Comptroller of the Currency that said Big Paul Castellano had a secret account at Franklin National Bank. You may have heard by now that the Vatican Bank lost $55 million when Franklin collapsed.

Sindona paid $6.5 million to Archbishop Paul Marcinkus, the chairman of the Vatican Bank, and to Roberto Calvi, the chairman of Banco Ambrosiano—supposedly for a stock price inflating scheme involving all three banks. He, Calvi and Marcinkus have smeared the reputations of the Vatican Bank and Banco Ambrosiano. People call Ambrosiano "the priests' bank;" this will reflect upon us.

There was more in the letter. Michael skimmed it, but saw nothing else that seemed relevant. Just news of other Society members that had nothing to do with banks or anything Father de Aragon had talked about yesterday. Michael picked up the next letter.

***

Vatican City, 3 January, 1975
Dear Paolo,

I send this letter with Father Greiner. I trust him. Fear rules in the Vatican. I've asked too many questions. Father Herzog cautions me to be careful, and I'm afraid he is right.

At first I thought Archbishop Marcinkus was unaware of Calvi's and Sindona's dishonesty. Anything else was too horrible to contemplate. But I think I was fooling myself. Marcinkus appears to be in it up to his collar.

Michael thought the setup was absurd. Archbishop Paul Casimir Marcinkus was a prominent man. Bishop of Orta, Chairman of the Vatican Bank, Chief of Vatican Intelligence and mayor of Vatican City. Having the same man head both the bank and the intelligence service was like the CIA running the Fed.

I've watched Marcinkus's career in fascination. How fitting that he was born in Cicero, the same Chicago suburb that gave us Al Capone. If he hadn't saved the life of the Holy Father Paul VI, he might not have risen to where he is now. I hear he is an avid golfer; after investigating the Vatican finances, I know how he keeps score.

I will say more when there is more to tell, if I can. In the meantime, pray for me.
Yours in Christ,
Mark

Michael set the letter down and reflected. What did he know about Marcinkus? Marcinkus organized Pope Paul VI's travel arrangements, his first big break in his rise through the Vatican bureaucracy. The Italian papers called the six-foot-four former rugby playing cleric "the Gorilla." He tackled a knife-wielding assassin who lunged at the Pope during a papal tour in the Philippines. In gratitude, the Pope made Marcinkus head of Vatican intelligence and security. Then, with Cardinal Spellman's backing, Marcinkus became Chairman of the Vatican Bank. That kind of power spawned a lot of temptation. With a heavy feeling in his gut, Michael went on to the next letter.

***

Milan, 20 November, 1978
Dear Paolo,

I'm deeply discouraged, and for the first time I'm frightened. I'm frightened for our Church, and I'm frightened for the honest and brave men who are helping us.

It seems longer than three years since I started working undercover in Banco Ambrosiano. It's been hard, but I've won Roberto Calvi's trust. The man makes my skin crawl.

I hoped Pope Paul VI's death would end this nightmare. Of course, I never wished death on our good Pope, but I hoped his successor would change things. Perhaps he would have, had he been spared.

I met with Albino Luciani, the Cardinal of Venice, before he became Pope John Paul I. Luciani was furious when Marcinkus sold the profitable Venetian Bank to Roberto Calvi.

I told Cardinal Luciani everything I knew. He was a good man. He vowed if he became Pope, he would put a stop to this corruption. He asked me to stay undercover in Banco Ambrosiano until such time as we could act. Almost as soon as he became John Paul I, he began asking questions. Questions I gave him, that made many powerful people in the Vatican uncomfortable. Vatican intelligence claimed he died of natural causes, but I wonder. Made Pope in August, dead in September after only thirty-three days. When I last saw him, he was in excellent health. And no one is asking uncomfortable questions any more.

I feel responsible, but also a little more hopeful than I did some weeks ago. Now that Karol Wojtyla has been elected Pope John Paul II, we may have another chance.

I talked to Father Herzog and Father Heilman. They urge me to continue my work, even though they fear for my safety. Father Herzog is organizing trustworthy men within the Society to fight this thing. I think he will be Superior General one day.

Father Herzog plans to visit you in South America next month. Listen to him. He is heartsick over the spiritual bankruptcy, the sexual and financial misconduct in the Church. He needs your help. I need your help.
Yours in Christ,
Mark

Michael recalled he had been in the United States at the time, and he'd heard vague rumors about John Paul I's death. But even knowing what he knew about corruption at the Vatican after seven frustrating years of investigating links between the Mafia and the Church, the rumors of murder were almost impossible to believe. Yet Marcinkus *had* sold the Venetian Bank to Roberto Calvi. And if Father Manion's judgment could be trusted, Cardinal Luciani had posed a threat to both men...and to their cronies.

***

Milan, 10 July, 1979
Dear Paolo,

The thieves are falling out. After Sindona was sentenced to twenty-five years in U.S. Federal prison, Calvi abandoned him and has forged new Italian Mafia links. Sindona wants revenge. He told the Italian banking authorities to investigate Calvi, especially his foreign corporations and links to the Vatican Bank.

Father Herzog reports the mood from the Vatican is grim. Marcinkus has more power than ever over religious promotions, money for bribes and Vatican internal surveillance. He surrounds himself with men motivated by greed and controlled by fear.

Pope John Paul II's election hasn't helped. As the first non-Italian Pope in more than four hundred years, Wojtyla was an outsider in the

Vatican power structure. A perfect target for Marcinkus to manipulate.

Marcinkus and the new Pope have become fast friends. They even resemble each other, both hulking Slavic men. Marcinkus was only too happy to help John Paul II find his power base; the old Italian power structure in the Vatican is gradually losing its control.

Marcinkus and Calvi are closer than ever. Marcinkus is untouchable. He reports directly to the Pope, and only to the Pope. The Pontiff protects him, and he protects Calvi. Even the Vatican Bank is becoming no more than Marcinkus's tool, apparently to aid Calvi in embezzling from Banco Ambrosiano's depositors. The bank set up dummy subsidiaries for Calvi's Luxembourg holding company in several countries, including Switzerland, Liechtenstein, Panama and the Bahamas. The subsidiaries are lending millions of Banco Ambrosiano's money to Panamanian corporations, while the Vatican Bank holds the stock as controlling fiduciary for Banco Ambrosiano. Officers at the Vatican Bank claim ignorance, of course...

The letter continued with more Vatican politics. Michael skipped this and went on to the next letter. The date was written American-style. A quick glance at the signature told him this one was from James.

***

Chicago, December 27, 1981
Dear Paolo,

I apologize for the delay, but I had to wait for a courier. Father Herzog and Father Manion have warned me to be careful.

In answer to your question, I think Father Manion can hold up to the pressure. He was in ragged shape when he arrived here, but it was only overwork and exhaustion.

It's hard to maintain a false identity. It's even harder to do it for years. Father Manion has an extraordinary strength of faith, character and self. He's in no danger mentally. It's the physical danger that concerns me.

The marked portion of the letter ended there. Michael stopped reading, with an unsettled feeling. James was mixed up in this, and clearly had been for years. He'd thought he knew everything about James, but now he realized he didn't know much at all.

The next two letters were from Father Manion. Michael noted this with a strange sense of relief.

***

Rome, 24 June, 1982
Dear Paolo,

This letter is a hard one to write. You will have heard by now of Roberto Calvi's death this past week. They are calling it a suicide, but it was murder. I watched it happen.

Calvi's fraud was on the brink of exposure, and he begged me to help him flee. We spent a week staying in safe houses all over Europe, then flew to London on 16 June. He was irrational, talking continually about his good friend Marcinkus and his own donations to Solidarnosc, the Pope's favorite cause. I feared for his sanity as well as his safety.

The night we arrived in London, we were in Calvi's hotel room. Calvi had stuffed his briefcase with incriminating documents and brought it with him. It was on the floor by his bed.

I heard a loud knock, and two rough-looking men entered. Calvi seemed to know them. They were Italian, though no names were spoken. Calvi vouched for me as a friend and officer of Banco Ambrosiano. The two men accepted that and told Calvi to come with them. Calvi insisted I come as well. I think he knew he wouldn't be coming back.

We drove to a boatyard, boarded a small boat and motored down the Thames. Calvi was nervous; he kept asking where they were taking us and when we would see Gelli. One of the men laughed and punched Calvi in the stomach. We had stopped by then, near Blackfriars Bridge. I took my chance and jumped over the side. I made it to the bank and hid. I wanted to keep running, but I knew I had to bear witness. So I stayed.

I saw everything. One of the men threw a rope over some scaffolding under the bridge, as if to make the boat fast. Then he wrapped the other end around Calvi's neck and stuffed something into Calvi's pockets. Rocks, the newspapers said later. The other man put the boat in gear and they sped off. The jolt snapped Calvi's neck. I cannot forget the sight of his corpse, swaying beneath the bridge.

I went back to the hotel, careful not to be seen. Calvi's briefcase was gone. The next day, the London papers said he had hanged himself under Blackfriars Bridge with a fat wad of cash and ten pounds of rocks in his pockets.

The men who killed Calvi easily could have killed me. They had guns; one shot is all it would have taken. I think they let me live as a witness. They killed Calvi because he mismanaged Mafia money, but he knew everything about their money-laundering operations and they wanted to shut his mouth. They also wanted to intimidate the P2.

I flew back to Rome the next day. I will never return to Banco Ambrosiano.

Michael was barely aware of his surroundings: the murmur of voices from outside his office, the minor physical discomfort from his recent bruises. He was absorbed in the world described by the handwritten pages.

***

Rome, 12 December, 1982
Dear Paolo,

Italian officials arrested Flavio Carboni, an officer of Banco Ambrosiano, trying to extort $900 thousand dollars from Vatican officials in exchange for Calvi's stolen documents. Bishop Pavel Hnilica was arrested trying to buy them back.

Hnilica—another Slav, like Marcinkus and John Paul himself—is part of Marcinkus's inner circle. Clandestine jokes about the Slavic Mafia are making the rounds in the Vatican, but the jokes stem from fear. No one knows what will happen next, only that it won't be good.

Banco Ambrosiano has officially collapsed, unable to survive the loss of the $1.3 billion Calvi looted from it with the assistance of the Vatican Bank. Licio Gelli's been arrested too. He was picked up in Switzerland while withdrawing $120 million from the Union Bank of Switzerland's Geneva branch. He entered the country on a false passport, and Switzerland has an extradition treaty with Italy. Thank God for technicalities. The Swiss are sending him back.

Marcinkus is claiming Calvi duped him. He's hiding in the Vatican, but he can't stay here forever. As soon as he steps off Vatican soil, he'll be arrested too. As to his defense, he may well get away with it. The corruption at the top has seeped throughout our clergy. Financial crimes here, sexual misconduct in the United States. We have much to answer for.

I told Father Herzog the past seven years had made me an old man. He said: "So if you had done something else, you think you wouldn't have grown old?" Typical Herzog. He has a point, but I would have grown old less quickly.
Yours in Christ,
Mark

Several years elapsed before the next letter. It was from James.

***

Rome, September 18, 1985
Dear Paolo,
Thank you again for your support. I'd no idea I'd create such a stir in the Vatican. Most people think I'm mad.

Obtaining permission to perform the exorcism almost required divine intervention. The Vatican administration felt it would seriously damage Catholic credibility if publicity about Jesuits performing exorcisms made the press and television news. Most priests view exorcism on par with hunting for leprechauns on St. Patrick's Day.

The Society granted approval in two days. The Vatican clergy grilled me for four. They asked me if I really believed in possession. I took your advice and told them that what was important was that the patients believed they were possessed.

Father Manion got a good chuckle out of my dilemma. He said I'd have much more support if I'd embezzled $100 million from the Vatican Bank. Speaking of which, Marcinkus is still hiding in the Vatican. I wonder how much longer he can stay here.

The Vatican Bank paid a $250 million settlement to the defrauded depositors of Banco Ambrosiano, but admitted nothing. What's most amazing to me is that Marcinkus raided the Vatican pension fund to come up with the money. Catholics have no idea where their donations are really going. Everyone involved with the scandal is still free. Father Manion finds that hard to accept. As do I.

I'll see you in Chicago next month.
Yours in Christ,
James

The next letter, posted from Chicago, came from Father Manion.

***

17 March, 1986
Dear Paolo,

James is finally out of the hospital. He's taken a few steps, and it's just a matter of time before he walks again. His features are recognizable, and he's making a fine and full recovery. Incredibly, his only permanent scars are from the back surgery and the teeth marks on his arm where he was bitten to the bone. The teeth missed a major artery by a millimeter.

I read your account and James's of the exorcism. I hope you won't attempt this treatment again.

James is actually happy with the result. His patient no longer believes himself possessed, and now James can treat what he calls the man's "garden variety" mental illness.

Despite the circumstances, it's good to be out of the Vatican. My mole in the Vatican Bank tells me he saw papers for another dummy corporation. The following week, $150 million appeared in the corporation's account. My mole thinks it's Latin American money. Any ideas?

Marcinkus isn't involved this time. The Pope tried to find a diplomatic post for him so he could leave the Vatican immune from prosecution, but so far hasn't succeeded. My only consolation is that Marcinkus can't play his beloved golf, and I hope he misses it. I plan to get in a few rounds

myself tomorrow. I'll send Marcinkus a postcard from the Oakbrook Country Club.
Yours in Christ,
Mark

The next two letters covered larger gaps in time, two and five years respectively.

***

Vatican City, 2 December, 1988
Dear Paolo,
Marcinkus got off scot-free. The authorities tried to indict him, but Italy's Supreme Court threw it out on grounds that the Vatican and its institutions enjoy sovereign status.

I sense Gelli's hand in this. The combination of the old P2 members and Mafia money bought too many top officials for these charges to stick to anyone.

A new generation of crooks infests the Vatican like rats. They call themselves the Archangeli. The Vatican Bank is laundering Italian Mafia money, and your hunch was correct. They're getting money from Colombia and other countries in Latin America as well. The documents are veiled in secrecy, but my mole is doing his best to get proof.
Yours in Christ,
Mark

The P2 and the Archangeli, Michael thought. The former, Italy's right-wing secret society; the latter, the same group of Mafia-linked clergy that the Specialists had been looking at for years with little to show for it. Licio Gelli had been P2's *Maestro Venerabile,* the Venerable Master.

Right-wing Freemasons, the members of P2, were wealthy Italian industrialists, publishers, high level military men and cops, and well placed politicians. An organized group of well-connected thugs, larcenous, lucrative and deadly. He kept reading.

***

Milan, 4 September, 1993
Dear Paolo,

Hard evidence and living witnesses both elude me. I pressured these men to help me, and now they're dead.

The papers reported Raul Gardini's murder as a suicide. The story referred to the Ca' Dario, a haunted Venetian castle with a long history of its owners meeting tragic ends. Gardini bought it in the eighties and now the "curse of the Haunted Palace" is being blamed for his death.

That's pure Gelli. He loves to scare his followers with this occult nonsense.

The truth is, Raul Gardini was about to give me evidence. He had proof of bribes and illegal money transfers out of Italy for the Italian Mafia this year.

Do you recall the stories about Ente Nazionale Idrocarburi, the Italian state energy corporation—the merger with Montedison, and the bribery scandal that followed? Gardini and Gabriele Cagliari, the head of ENI, were indicted for it. Gardini had nothing more to lose, so he agreed to help me if I used my influence to lighten his sentence. Cagliari agreed to the same deal.

The day before he would have been arrested, Gardini's body was found in his apartment. Cagliari died in his prison cell in Milan. No chance of suicide being blamed for that one; he was asphyxiated by a plastic bag over his head. His killers couldn't have been more obvious if they had put a bullet in his brain.

I may be next, unless I am very careful. I don't plan to leave the Vatican until this is over. The Society's power protects me here.
Yours in Christ,
Mark

Poor Father Manion, Michael thought. The Society *had* protected him, but not for long enough.

CHAPTER IX

Vatican City
Monday, June 17

By the time Michael finished reading, he had just enough time to find a caffe and have a sandwich and espresso and still get to the Vatican by 3:00 p.m. A brief detour to the library set him back an extra ten minutes, but he should still make it. His head was spinning with everything he'd learned, though he didn't yet see how it tied into the murders of Father Manion and Father Pintozzi. Whatever hard evidence Father Herzog had of who was behind the notorious crimes from the past or the current murders, he owed it to Father Manion's courage. After reading the letters, Michael felt as if he knew the man, and badly wanted to bring his killers to justice.

Father James was waiting for him outside the Jesuit apartments, and greeted him in English. "I hope I'm not late." Michael appraised his friend with fresh eyes. He'd known James for almost two decades, yet after reading the letters he realized he knew very little about James.

"You're right on time."

Michael matched James's pace. They moved swiftly around the colonnade to the right of the basilica. Two Swiss guards stopped them at the base of the Scala Regia, the royal staircase designed by Bernini in the 1600s. In their orange and navy striped uniforms with billowing pantaloons and puffed sleeves, their heads crowned by black berets, they resembled large menacing dolls. Their expressions were grim, unyielding. The Vatican was still on red alert after Saturday's murder.

Although Father James wore a cassock, the guards did not relax until they checked his identification and compared his face with his photo. They asked for Michael's identification as well, then finally nodded and stood aside.

A little further up the staircase was an archway crowned by the papal insignia: keys, papal crown and crest. Two angels supported the insignia on either side, blowing trumpets with their free hands as if announcing the visitors. Two more rows of columns, each flanked by another pair of Swiss guards, supported the archway itself. The guards looked gravely at them and waved them through.

"How large are the Jesuit apartments?" Michael asked.

"Not very. Most Jesuits don't live in the Vatican, only a few very highly placed leaders of the Society."

They walked through echoing marble halls and finally turned into a smaller hallway carpeted by a wide Persian runner. As they halted before the third door on the left, a young priest stepped out of an alcove, knocked on the door and opened it.

"Father James Talman has arrived," the younger man said into the room beyond.

A clear voice answered in Italian. "Wonderful. Show him in."

Michael followed James into the large comfortable-looking study. As with Father de Aragon at Michael's apartment the other day, the air felt oddly dense and warm, yet comforting. A soft hum, so low he could barely hear it, added to the soothing effect. He had the sensation of being watched—no, more than watched. Probed, with an intensity that almost unnerved him, by the other two men in the room.

Seeking distraction, he glanced around. The room looked like a much larger version of his own study, minus the desk and computer equipment. Overstuffed reading chairs were positioned on a large oriental carpet in the middle of the room.

The feeling of probing intensity ebbed. He turned his attention to the two unfamiliar priests. Both elderly men looked delighted to see James. Father James greeted them with warm handclasps, then turned to Michael. "This is Father Herzog, the Superior General."

"It's a pleasure to meet you, Father Herzog." He nodded toward the man, observing him in turn. Herzog stood straight and tall, as if he were decades younger. His slender frame looked wiry and muscular, and his sharp grey eyes missed nothing. Michael had taken a little extra time to do his homework before coming here; he knew Herzog had been elected to his high office just six months prior and was a descendant of a wealthy noble German family.

Herzog gestured to James to take the empty chair next to him, then turned to Michael and smiled. "We are most grateful you agreed to meet with us. May we speak in English?"

"Yes." Michael preferred English for analytical thinking. Although he loved the beauty and expressiveness of Italian, English lent itself better to reason and logic. He had a feeling both would be needed here today.

Father Herzog turned toward the other unfamiliar priest—another man in his eighties, shorter than Herzog but giving off a similar air of vigor. "This is my aide, Father Heilman."

"My pleasure." Michael bent slightly as he shook the man's hand, noting Heilman's steel grey-hair and enigmatic expression.

"And mine." Father Heilman gripped Michael's hand firmly, looking him directly in the eyes.

They sat down, Michael directly across from Father Herzog. "So why did you ask me here?" Michael said.

"First, let me make something clear," Father Herzog said. "We do not represent the Church. At least, not yet."

"No," was all Michael could think to say. He glanced at James, but his old friend's serene expression yielded no information.

Father Herzog went on. "We represent the Society of Jesus and our Rota."

Michael knew what that was. "But there is no Rota," he said. "The Rota was the ancient ecclesiastical court. Nowadays the Vatican has its own civil court, and the tribunal of the Church cardinals deals with internal Church matters."

A slight smile crossed Herzog's face. "Your trip to the library was not wasted."

"You had me watched?" Michael spoke sharply, with another glance at James that earned him nothing.

"Yes," Father Herzog replied. "For your own protection."

"And the photographer this morning?"

Herzog looked puzzled, and somewhat alarmed. "I'm sorry. Could you explain that?"

Michael did. He also explained the added security he had put around his villa. All three priests listened with heightened interest. James leaned forward, looking deeply concerned.

"We had nothing to do with that," Father Herzog said firmly. "We do not condone violence or invade people's homes. We only tracked your whereabouts, as you may be in danger."

He ignored that for the moment. In his line of work, he was used to being in danger. "Then who did?"

"Probably the Archangeli."

117

Michael gave a slight nod, accepting his answer. He'd thought of that possibility himself. "So what is the Rota?"

"The Rota is a new court founded within the Jesuit community." Father Herzog paused. "We intend to use it to take over the administration of the Catholic Church."

Stunned, Michael was tempted to ask if he had heard correctly. No wonder James had been unwilling to talk about it. The Jesuits were powerful in their own way, but had never been part of the religious clique that ran the Church. They had worked largely unimpeded for centuries because they avoided just this sort of conflict. Yet Father Herzog had just announced his intention to supplant the very authority that could disband the Jesuits. He shook his head. "You'll be excommunicated. Not just the three of you; the entire order." Yet even as he said it, he felt a flare of hope. If they succeeded...

"I will meet with the Pope on Friday," Father Herzog continued. "He will continue as spiritual leader, of course."

For a few moments Michael was speechless. "And if the Pope does not go along with your plan?" he said finally.

"Then we will have lost everything."

Michael still couldn't believe it. This would cause the biggest upheaval in the Catholic Church in centuries. Could they pull it off? It didn't' seem possible. Michael leaned forward. "You're risking your life's work and the global

Jesuit community. Why are you doing this? Why now?"

"Because the Catholic Church is dying from the evil within." Father Herzog's face turned profoundly sad. "The number of men studying to be priests has dropped to one-third of what it was forty years ago. In Europe, the average age of priests is over 65. In the United States, major contributors have cut off funds out of disgust over sex abuse charges and the Church's cover-ups. We must challenge these evils and take action against them."

"But why now?" Michael asked. "There have been scandals in the Church for centuries. Yet you intend to move within days."

Father Herzog glanced at Father Heilman and James. "We are in imminent danger of exposure," he said. "Two weeks ago, a member of the Rota—Father Mark Manion—was killed before he could testify against top leaders in the Vatican. This past Saturday, Father Matteo Pintozzi was killed in the Vatican Museum. He was our mole in the Archangeli. The leaders of the Vatican surely know that, which means we are nearly out of time."

"Father Manion and Father Pintozzi were collecting evidence? What sort of evidence?"

"We can implicate many high-level administrators of the Catholic Church in sexual and financial misconduct that would earn them long prison sentences or worse," Herzog said. "The Catholic Church in the United States is in deep financial trouble. Everyone knows about the huge financial judgments against us to settle sexual abuse cases; what isn't known is how much of the scandal we repressed. As more payments are required, we will lose more schools, more churches and more land. We may even become insolvent."

Shock flooded through Michael. He knew the situation in the United States was bad, but this meant the death of the Catholic Church in North America. Contributions were down, along with enrollments in the priesthood. But instead of fixing the problem, the Church was throwing money at it. The Church spent $102 billion a year just on its U.S. operations; it couldn't afford the drop in donations compounded by expensive lawsuits. Three U.S. dioceses had already gone bankrupt because of the sex abuse cases.

Father Herzog continued. "The Archangeli are desperate for money. In the past, they laundered money for the Mafia and European embezzlers. After the Banco Ambrosiano scandal, they curtailed their illegal financial operations, but now they are up to their old tricks and they have turned to aiding tax evaders. As a sovereign state, the Vatican is offshore with respect to the rest of Europe. The Archangeli use additional offshore vehicles in the Caymans so the cash is untraceable."

"You have proof?" Michael asked.

"Yes. I'm prepared to confront the Pope. But we may not prevail."

Michael let out a slow breath. Father Herzog, the Superior General of the Society of Jesus, intended to blackmail the Pope. He couldn't help admiring the man's audacity. But it meant taking a terrible risk.

Within the Vatican, I have no jurisdiction. What can I do?"

"We'll give you the evidence to prosecute high-level clerics in the Vatican, and we want that evidence made public as soon as possible."

Michael shook his head. "I cannot press charges while these priests are inside the Vatican."

Father Herzog nodded. "First we'll excommunicate them. Then we'll expel the offenders from Vatican soil and you can prosecute them under Italian law. We also have evidence implicating high-level Italian industrialists, political leaders and Mafia leaders. You will have it all."

The prospect dazzled Michael. All these years of fruitless effort, and now these three brave men—along with all those who had helped them—were offering to drop a miracle into his lap. "There's just one thing," he said. "The killings of Father Manion and Father Pintozzi may mean that the Archangeli have a mole within the Rota."

Father Herzog's eyes grew bright, as if with unshed tears. "Yes," he agreed. "We believe we've been betrayed."

"By Father Pintozzi?"

"No." Father Herzog sounded vehement. "We know he was loyal. We think it is a member of Father Pleurre's code group. Perhaps Pleurre himself, or Father Graf, or Father de Aragon. Father Pintozzi never met the leader, but the Archangeli gave him a high-level Jesuit code to access our computer files. They didn't know he was our mole. We only allowed infiltration of the lowest level files, and we did not inform Father Pleurre of our plan."

"But if Father Pleurre has access to the information anyway, how can you suspect him?"

"We wanted to see his reaction. Father Pleurre is head of our finances and our computer security. He is brilliant, and may have been testing Father Pintozzi to see if he would turn over valuable information to the Archangeli. If Father Pleurre turned over the information himself, it would be instantly traced back, but using Father Pintozzi as a blind conduit would avert suspicion."

"What about the others?"

"Both Father Graf and Father de Aragon know enough about our systems and finances to do the same thing. Father Pleurre encoded critical information, but he used the code developed in his group. Only his code group and mine have access to our passwords. The truth is, we don't know who is guilty."

"But you have a plan to find out."

"Not anymore. Matteo was our only mole. We fed some good information to the Archangeli so they would believe in his sincerity. Only the priests in this room knew he was our mole, and now you know."

Michael looked at the three men. Father Heilman and Father Herzog were the leaders of the Society of Jesus and of the Rota. It was a testament to their high regard for James that they trusted only him with their most sensitive secrets. Michael knew they were only revealing so much to an outsider because they had no other choice, and because James vouched for him.

"After we clean up the mess in the Vatican, we'll give foreign authorities dossiers on other wrongdoers that we've 'borrowed' from various religious orders. Criminals will no longer hide behind the robes of the Church." Father Herzog's gaze bored into him. Michael once again had the feeling of being probed, only much stronger this time. His head began to throb slightly.

"Will you help us?" Herzog asked.

Michael hesitated. He needed the Jesuits as much as they needed him. The Specialists had worked for over a decade to get hard evidence on the men involved in the Vatican Bank scandals, yet the culprits were still free and up to their old tricks of bribery, embezzlement, and violent vendettas. If Michael agreed to help the Jesuits, he'd finally get the evidence he needed.

He also knew Father Herzog was right about the Church. Michael had lost much of his own faith after Irena died, but the Jesuits had given back enough to keep him going. He found, to his surprise, that the fate of the Church mattered to him. If the Jesuits took it over, the Church would come back to its better self. The Jesuits weren't perfect, but they were fundamentally good men. Jesuits had taught Michael how to think independently. He owed them that, and for helping him learn to go on living after Irena's death.

He looked at James, who sat expressionless, as if willing Michael to make his own decision. Then he met Father Herzog's gaze. "I will help you," he said.

Father Herzog relaxed and he nodded with visible relief. "Then James will introduce you to Father Pleurre. He can give you all the information we have on what we've discussed."

"Can I trust him?" Michael asked.

"To an extent, yes. But keep your eyes open." Father Herzog rose to leave, and Father Heilman followed suit. "You must excuse us now."

The departing priests stood straight and moved easily, as if they were decades younger. They looked as if they had lived a life hiking in the mountains instead of running a holy order. Michael realized they must practice both a strict mental and physical regimen. He turned to James. "Let's go."

CHAPTER X

Vatican City
Monday, June 17

James shepherded Michael out the door, through the reception area to another room filled with computers. A priest about the same age as Father de Aragon, mid-fifties or so, stood in the center of the room. He glanced around, saw James, and hurried over with a frown. "This is Visconte, then?" he said, eying Michael suspiciously. He had the distinguished look of an elderly French duke, right down to the petulant expression of a nobleman forced to deal with peasants.

"This is Father Pleurre," James said, ignoring his fellow priest's rudeness. "He can show you what you need to know."

Michael nodded. "The first thing I want to see is the last trade Father Matteo Pintozzi executed."

Father Pleurre looked ready to protest. Father James's genial expression didn't change, and after a moment, Father Pleurre gave a sharp sigh. "This way," he said.

Michael and James followed him down another corridor. James murmured an explanation as they walked: "Father Pleurre tracks the revenues coming into and leaving the Society through the work of the global Jesuit community. Donations and estate gifts from the faithful are also included. Networks of corporations controlled by the Society keep the true ownership of these funds out of the public eye."

They reached a set of carved wooden double doors. Two Swiss guards stood on either side. They clearly recognized the priests and swung the heavy doors open, then closed them after the three men walked through.

They crossed a small inner chamber and went toward another set of doors, this one flanked by two young Jesuit priests seated on chairs and working on laptops. "Another precaution," James explained. "These priests ensure that only authorized Jesuits enter the computer area. High-ranking Vatican clergy might be able to get past the Swiss guards, but not past these two."

He gave them a signal, and the priest on the left opened the inner set of doors. The room beyond contained five rectangular tables supporting dozens of computers, screens and printers.

Father Pleurre approached a table in the middle. "This was Father Matteo's workstation. If you give me a moment, I will access his last trade." Still looking reluctant, the priest tapped out a series of keystrokes. Then he stepped back.

Michael moved forward and peered at the screen. Father Pintozzi had done a classic hedge fund trade, a convertible arbitrage. The arbitrage involved a relatively unknown Spanish company, Resorts Azore. They were building a new hotel. Three years earlier, the price of the stock had dropped to 16 euros per share. At that time, Matteo bought warrants giving him the right to buy the shares at a price of 40 euros. The warrants were selling for almost nothing, about 0.25 euros, since the odds of the shares rising above 40 euros were slim. Matteo's computer model said the warrants should be worth about 5 euros, given the volatility in the stock price. Matteo had bought all one million warrants, all that were available, for a cost of 250,000 euros and hedged by selling short 74,000 shares of Resorts Azore stock at 16 euros per share.

Smart move, Michael thought. Theoretically Matteo was hedged and also had instant income. Then a year after Pintozzi put on the trade, the stock dropped below 2 euros per share. Matteo bought back the 74,000 shares he had shorted for a total cost of 2 euros apiece, including fees and expenses, locking in a profit of 1,036,000 euros. Subtracting the original cost of the warrants left him with a net profit of 786,000 euros, and Matteo still owned the warrants free and clear. After that, Resorts Azore issued debt and expanded. It became the go-to destination for wealthy Europeans and Latin Americans. The stock soared. Just before he died, Matteo had sold the warrants for 98 euros each net of fees and expenses, making 98,000,000 million euros. On the combined trades, Pintozzi made 98,786,000 euros in three years on an initial out-of-pocket investment of only 250,000 euros: a phenomenal average annual return of 633 percent per year.

"I wish I had known Father Pintozzi," Michael said. "Was this typical? And how did he do it? No model can predict these results."

Father Pleurre shrugged. "This was an unusually profitable transaction. The bulk of his trades had annual returns of more than 42 percent and some of them much more. Occasionally, very rarely, we lose money on a trade. Most of our trades are very profitable, and our annualized returns have been quite large."

Michael frowned at the computer screen. He had hoped to discover that Matteo was losing money. That might have been a motive for murder. This didn't make any sense. Who would want to kill the golden goose?

"Did he do any naked short selling?" Michael was casting about for anything that might shed some light.

Pleurre actually sneered. "I'm not saying he did, but I'll remind you that the Vatican is a sovereign state, and there is no law against it here."

Michael knew he was intelligent, if not quite a match for Father Pintozzi, with an excellent education in mathematics and finance.

Computers tended to be a great equalizer, too. Yet he couldn't have pulled off a transaction record like Pintozzi's. "How did he manage to consistently make such profits?" he murmured, almost to himself.

James spoke up then, his voice low. "Father Pintozzi had a singular advantage," he said. "Years ago, Father Herzog translated an obscure work written in Russian by Daniel Bernoulli in 1738. Bernoulli said risky ventures should be evaluated using the geometric mean, not the arithmetic mean of the outcomes. Father Pintozzi understood what this meant and based his work for the Society on it."

"Meaning?"

"Suppose you can make a bet in the markets. You start out with $1 billion, and the outcomes are that you could end up with either zero or $2 billion. If you try to predict the outcome using the arithmetic mean, the expected value of your portfolio is zero plus $2 billion divided by two, or $1 billion. This answer is not useful. Would you make a bet with $1 billion knowing you might lose it all?"

"No," Michael said.

"The geometric mean gives you a more sensible answer. You compute it by multiplying the outcomes and taking the number of outcomes as the root. In this case, since there are only two outcomes, you take the square root of $2 billion times zero. Since zero times anything is zero, the expected value is zero. A competent money manager would be crazy to make this bet, but Father Pintozzi was intrigued with the idea of assessing the odds of a payoff and scaling the investment based on the likelihood of a favorable outcome and the size of the portfolio. When he decided on a choice of trades, he always chose investments with the highest geometric mean of outcomes."

"Even with a computer model, I don't see how he could be this consistent and this profitable for six years," Michael said.

Father Pleurre gave him an enigmatic smile. "You are correct. The real investment world is too complicated to be reduced to a model."

"Then how did he pick his trades?"

The smile became a smirk. "That was mostly my invention."

"Your invention?"

"I showed you what you wanted to see," Father Pleurre said. "Now—"

A voice, clipped and tense, came from across the room. "Our visitor's back."

James hurried over to where the speaker was, by the main computer banks. A dark-haired priest in his mid-thirties sat in front of a large computer screen. He pointed. James muttered something under his breath, then called for Michael to come over. Father Pleurre hung back, his mouth a thin line.

"Here's where we have the problem," James said as Michael reached him. He nodded toward the computer screen. "Someone's trying to break into our data files. Clever little demon. Clever enough to be a Jesuit."

Michael turned his attention to the screen, where lines of code had spontaneously appeared. He frowned at them. "This isn't the work of an ordinary hacker. What's the security like on your system?"

Security was the best available, James explained. The Society never used a public access data superhighway, since a good hacker could pirate passwords and invade a user's computer network. The Society kept its own financial databases as well as cataloguing everything the Jesuit Society learned. Catholic record keeping ate up another huge chunk of memory. E-mail was the weakest link, but sensitive information was always sent in code. Often, the Jesuits had better political intelligence than the CIA.

As an added safeguard, the Society coded each priest's password information so other priests on the network could not view it. Even Jesuit hackers couldn't get each other's passwords. "We're protected by a Byzantine labyrinth," James concluded. "You almost need a guided code to find your way out of it. Father Pintozzi gave the Archangeli access to the two lowest of the seven security clearance levels. Our intruder is accessing that level now."

"I know how to find him," Michael said. "In fact, I'll turn the tables and go after the intruder's system. Two can play this game."

"How?" James asked.

"We arrested a super-hacker for computer espionage a while back, and he turned counterintelligence to escape sentencing. He taught me the latest techniques for catching corporate computer raiders." Michael pulled a thumb drive off of his key ring and turned to the dark-haired priest whose workstation this was. "May I?"

The man nodded and moved aside. Michael sat down and began working. "I'm setting up a bait file peppered with the kind of information the intruder was after, plus some bonuses," he said. "When he takes the bait, he'll carry a counter-invasion program back to his own system. As soon as he logs off, I'll log on to his system and raid his files."

"But what if we bring back a virus or a Trojan?" The voice was Father Pleurre's; Michael hadn't seen him come up. The priest frowned and fidgeted. Was it just that he disapproved of outsiders being here, or was there more to it?

"I'm setting up a dedicated protected area to isolate the intruder's entire software system when I download it. It'll only be a copy, but we'll have the whole thing, not just some level-two data. I can scrub his software for viruses and worms. I won't risk contaminating your system."

They watched as the intruder's worm moved closer to the hook. As Michael had hoped, the hacker took the bait.

"Gotcha!" Michael said, grinning.

He waited until the intruder logged off, then reestablished the link. Next, he turned toward the screen to his right and used his password code-breaking algorithms to log on to the intruder's system. He then typed in command after command to break through every level of the intruder's security. Whoever it was, they were good. Very good. But not good enough.

It took Michael two hours to copy the intruder's system, about an hour longer than he had planned. Fortunately, the intruder did not return to log on. Once satisfied he had everything, Michael removed all evidence of his invasion and logged off the intruder's system.

"We got it all," he said with a smile. He sat back and gave a long, satisfied stretch.

James smiled broadly. Even Father Pleurre looked impressed.

"So what have we got?" James asked.

Michael got up. "First thing tomorrow, we'll examine it and find out."

***

Michael went back to the Vatican Museum and retraced the steps Father Matteo Pintozzi had taken two days before. As he'd feared, the priest must have been murdered within a few minutes of Helena's finding him.

He went back to St. Peter's Square to plan his next move. He gazed up at the basilica as if it might hold the answer. When he looked back at the priests, nuns and tourists milling in the square, he saw a familiar figure. The young woman whose purse had been snatched just yesterday stood less than fifty feet in front of him. Her long golden hair and brown eyes reminded him of Irena. She even wore a blue dress. The resemblance hit him hard enough to ache.

She noticed him staring at her and frowned slightly. Michael looked away, feeling heat rise in his cheeks. He imagined what she must think: *another Italian gigolo.* From the corner of his eye, he saw her walking towards him.

"It's you!" she said. "Thank you for helping me the other day. I'm Susan Chambers. I'm a freelance reporter writing a travel piece on the Vatican."

Susan, not Irena. American, not Italian. Alive, not dead. A sudden, vivid memory of her clutching him after the purse-snatching made his stomach twist into knots. With difficulty, he kept his voice and gaze steady and polite. The thought crossed his mind that her hair should be red instead of blonde, but he brushed the thought aside.

"I'm Michael Visconte." He heard himself going on, though part of him knew he shouldn't. "I'm very familiar with the Vatican. Perhaps I can be of some help."

Susan smiled. "You're an American! I didn't pick up on the accent the other day."

"Not exactly," Michael corrected her. "My mother was an American, and I studied there."

She stepped back and let her gaze travel over his face and clothes. He hoped she liked what she saw. He was fit, he knew, from running, weight training and a rigorous martial arts program he practiced four times a week. Women generally found him good-looking, though his features were marred by an uneven nose that he owed to a couple of breaks suffered in the line of duty.

He retreated to what he knew best. "What happened to you the other day? Why didn't you wait for me?"

"The purse only held some cash; my passport and credit cards were in my hotel safe. I was frightened, and I didn't know who you were," Susan said.

"Do you always throw your arms around strangers?" Michael turned his head away, surprised at himself for flirting with her.

She smiled at him. Her head was almost level with his chin. "No. I must have been in shock."

"You were in luck. I work for the Italian police. Though I specialize in financial crimes, not running down purse-snatchers." He told himself he was trying to put her at ease, but he knew he was trying to impress her with his authority and hoped he didn't sound pompous.

"You're right. It was my lucky day." She smiled and took his arm. "I'll buy you an espresso if you'll answer a few questions, Mr. Expert on the Vatican."

Something in her posture reminded him of Irena—the way she'd looked in an old photo Michael kept. For an instant, it struck him as a pose. Then the impression passed. He regarded her thoughtfully. Her invitation carried no undertones beyond simple friendliness. Even so, he felt a thrill of anticipation.

"On one condition," he said.

"Yes?"

"I'll buy the espressos. I know just the place."

She let out an easy laugh. "A dinosaur! I accept."

CHAPTER XI

Vatican City
Monday, June 17

Michael led her to a café off a side street near the Vatican. Unlike the cafés on the main tourist drag, this one was clean with fresh-cut flowers and sparkling marble table tops. Michael held out a chair for Susan and sat facing her. Then he flagged a waiter, and their espressos arrived without delay.

"I just changed some money at the Vatican Bank," Susan said. "Creepy place. It's so dark, and all those clerics working behind the counters, whispering. I've never seen anything like it. Didn't I read something about a guy at the Vatican Bank who killed himself? Not recently; years ago. I think it was in London, though."

"Roberto Calvi," Michael said. "He was found hanging under Blackfriars Bridge in London in 1982." He paused and finished his espresso, then decided to continue. "He was murdered. They called it suicide at the time, even though almost everyone suspected foul play. About twenty years later, advanced forensic techniques proved he was murdered, but it was impossible to tell exactly how after all that time." He thought of the harrowing description in Father Manion's letter, but kept it to himself. The priest could have told the authorities quite a bit, had he lived to do so.

"Gruesome." Susan shivered, but he still saw curiosity in her face. She was so young. She hadn't even been born when Calvi was killed.

"So why was Calvi murdered?" Susan asked.

"Money. Calvi was the head of Banco Ambrosiano in Milan. He masterminded the embezzlement of $1.3 billion from the bank's depositors. The sad part was, the bank handled mostly private family deposits, and many people saw their life savings wiped out. The Italian courts linked the murder to the Mafia, but couldn't prove it."

"What did the Vatican Bank have to do with it?"

"This gets complicated. Are you sure you want to hear it?"

She leaned forward, resting one elbow on the table and her chin in her hand. "I'm fascinated. Please go on."

"All right." He was enjoying himself, a welcome change from the stress of the past few days. "As controlling fiduciary for Banco Ambrosiano, the Vatican Bank held shares in offshore dummy corporations. In one transaction, Banco Ambrosiano Lima deposited money with the Vatican Bank. When the Lima branch wanted its deposit back, the Vatican Bank claimed they didn't have to pay, that the dummy corporation owed the money, even though the

Vatican Bank controlled the dummy corporation."

"Then what happened?"

"The money disappeared. The administrator, Banco Gottardo, said they took instructions from Roberto Calvi, even though the Vatican Bank was the controlling fiduciary. Which means that at the very least, the Vatican Bank was an enabler."

He flagged a waiter, and they placed their orders. After the waiter left, Michael said, "But you didn't come here to talk about the Vatican scandals. You mentioned a travel piece?"

"I was thinking of that. You know, nothing heavy, just something to justify this trip. But now..."

"Then allow me to give you a tour of the basilica."

Michael put some money on the table, and they walked out of the cafe towards the piazza of Pius XII. They were just east of the Vatican city limits, next to some souvenir shops. Due west lay the piazza of Saint Peter, the most photographed piazza in the world, just in front of its namesake basilica. Tour buses and taxi cabs clogged the square.

Michael led Susan into the piazza and pointed out landmarks as they faced the basilica. In the center was a huge obelisk with large fountains on either side. A colonnade encircled the piazza, each column crowned with a triple life-sized statue of a Pope or an apostle. Atop the left and right sides of the basilica were even larger statues of Saint Peter and Saint Paul.

"These statues may not be here in a hundred years unless we take some measures to protect them," Michael said.

"Protect them from what?"

"Pollution, mainly. There's a lot of erosion, too. When we get up there later, you'll see what I mean. The statues look like chalk figures dissolving in the rain."

"But these statues have been here a long time."

"Yes, but only in recent times has pollution been this bad in Rome." He gave her a wry smile. "People don't use catalytic converters here like they do in the United States."

"Are you married?" Susan asked suddenly.

The question caught him flat-footed. "Yes." And then, to his own surprise, he added, "But that doesn't mean I'm dead. The world holds a lot of attractive distractions." His gaze swept over her, and he felt his cheeks grow warm.

Susan laughed softly. "I've noticed you've noticed."

He guided her to Bernini's staircase, which led to the entrance of the church. A scantily clad young woman was being turned away by a guard. Michael eyed Susan's outfit, a knee-length sleeveless blue silk dress that tied halter style at the neck and exposed part of her back. He shrugged off his jacket and held it out to her. "Here. You'd better put this on."

"Why?"

"They won't let you in dressed like you are. Not even if you were the Pope's sister. Women aren't allowed to wear shorts, or anything sleeveless or backless. Only in recent years have they let women enter without a head covering. Men have to be appropriately dressed, too."

"And I thought the Italians were so liberal."

He chuckled. "There is an old saying: In America everything is allowed, except that which is forbidden. In Germany everything is forbidden, except that which is allowed. In Italy everything is allowed, especially that which is forbidden. But in the Vatican, everything is forbidden, even that which is allowed."

Susan laughed. "And we are in the Vatican." She looked at him impishly and then said, "Just wait until we get back to Italy."

Her remark disconcerted him, so he pretended he hadn't heard the invitation in her tone. "The Vatican really is its own country. Don't be fooled just because you don't need your passport to get inside. The Vatican has its own rules."

He draped his suit jacket around her, letting his hands linger on her shoulders a moment longer than necessary. She gave him a flirtatious glance, and they walked past the Vatican guard who nodded his head in approval. They marched up the short flight of sweeping stone steps, through the open doors, and into the wide outer entrance hall of Saint Peter's Basilica.

Susan gasped, and Michael laughed inwardly at her reaction. The ceiling was adorned with frescoes. Every centimeter of ceiling, wall and floor was decorated with carved marble, mosaics, gilt or Renaissance paintings. As always, Michael felt something that had nothing to do with faith in God or spirituality. What he felt was a sense of enormous power. St. Peter's seemed less a house of God than a testament to the far-reaching clout of the Catholic Church.

"Religion in your face," Susan said. "It's breathtaking."

All around them, tourists snapped pictures. Michael spotted Chinese, Japanese, Arabs, Africans and an assortment of Europeans. He gestured at the surrounding walls. "Here you see the artwork of Michelangelo, Bernini, Carlo Fontana, Giacomo Della Porta, Donatello, Algardi, Canova, Francesco Messina, Vignola and scores of others," he said. "Just let me know if I'm going too fast."

"I'll never remember all the names," Susan said.

"Don't worry. Everyone feels like that the first time. Just try to get the flavor of the art. You can come back at your leisure and examine your favorite pieces. I'll give you an official Vatican guide book with my compliments." He grinned again. "I've been here many times, and each time I see something I didn't notice before."

"All this must be worth a fortune."

"Priceless," Michael agreed. "And this is just a drop in the ocean. The Church likes to keep quiet about it, but they have the largest real estate holdings of any institution or individual in the world. Prime real estate in major cities, even agricultural holdings. Land bought with donations from the faithful, land donated for churches and labor donated to build them, land willed upon the death of the faithful, land donated for schools. Two millennia of donations. Tax free."

"And there are churches and schools on all that land?"

"Hardly. The church collects a lot of rent from apartment buildings, even parking lots."

"But the Church always cries poor," Susan said. "Why not sell some of it?"

"Good question," he said dryly.

He steered her over to the far right near the doors. This was the chapel of the Pietà, which housed Michelangelo's famous white marble statue of the Virgin holding the corpse of the crucified Jesus. Even though he had seen it many times, Michael was affected by the sight of the mourning woman holding her son's body. The limp figure of Jesus seemed to melt into the folds of her robe.

He next led Susan to the bronze statue of Saint Peter by Arnolfo di Cambio. The foot of the statue was almost worn away, kissed or touched in devotional reverence by visitors to the basilica.

"The foot is frequently replaced, and it's due for another," Michael said. He took her hand and placed it on the line around the ankle, where the foot had been severed and reattached.

The church was clotted with more paintings and a seemingly endless supply of small chapels and statues of saints. Mosaics replicating other famous paintings crowded the view. Michael suggested they skip the art gallery on the left-hand side of the basilica. "There are crypts underneath the Vatican. A whole network of tunnels where early Christians and saints and generations of Popes are buried. Would you like to see them?"

"No thanks," Susan said quickly. "I'll come back on Halloween."

Michael laughed. He felt twenty again. "In that case, let's look at the view from the dome."

"I'd love to see it. And I'd be grateful for some fresh air. The atmosphere is overwhelming."

They walked out of the basilica and made a hard left in the entrance hall. Another left took them past a souvenir shop, which Michael said they would visit after seeing the view from the dome. Tourists with cameras milled everywhere, snapping pictures of everything in sight, including the souvenir shop's display windows. Michael led Susan straight ahead toward a long line of tourists.

"It will take forever to see the dome," Susan groaned.

"Not today." Michael guided her by the elbow to the front of the line, where he produced a large euro note. The attendant ushered them in. They climbed up 300 steps, then entered a gallery that encircled the inside of the dome and looked down at a panoramic view of the interior.

"From up here, the basilica doesn't look quite so formidable. It looks more like a postcard," Susan said.

They climbed up another 300 or so steps and exited to another gallery that encircled the dome's exterior.

Michael gave a slight bow and gestured to the view below. "All of Rome is at your feet." Tourists with cameras circled throughout the gallery, so intent on taking pictures that Michael wondered if they took time to enjoy the view. One man in particular hovered near him and Susan, snapping pictures first to their right and then to their left.

Michael looked down at Saint Peter's square. From this high up, the ant-like figures of visitors looked like colorful moving dots. The layout of the architecture drew his gaze through the square and down the wide Via Conciliazione to the Tiber. He shielded his eyes from the sun and looked at the dark angel at the top of Castel Sant'Angelo, just slightly off center and to the left. He could see the Seven Hills of Rome and all the major landmarks.

Susan pulled a map out of her handbag. "Help me find the monuments."

He gladly complied. They had only just met, but he felt an overwhelming desire to be alone with her. He pushed thoughts of Helena firmly to the back of his mind. He rested an arm around Susan's shoulder as he pointed to the map and then touched her cheek as he directed her gaze at the city below.

"Now let me show you the Vatican gardens." He took her hand and they walked around the dome to where the gardens were. Just beyond lay the Vatican museum's exterior courtyards. He thought of Father Matteo Pintozzi, then felt annoyed with himself for letting darkness intrude.

Susan turned to Michael with an appraising look. "You don't take religion very seriously, do you?"

He replied with an enigmatic smile and a verse:

> *"The hand that rounded Peter's dome*
> *And groined the aisles of ancient Rome*
> *Wrought in a sad sincerity*
> *Himself from God he could not free."*

Susan frowned, as if uncertain. "What's that supposed to mean?"

"It's a quote from Emerson's poem, 'The Problem.' "But to answer your question, I'm not entirely sure what I believe in."

She looked at him intently, but said nothing.

They descended the staircase to the passageway that led to the gift shop. "I need to buy some souvenirs," Susan said.

"Then you've come to the right place." Michael opened the shop door for her. "The Catholic Church means business."

The shop displayed rosaries made of faux pearls, garnets, aurora borealis, carved wood, carved coral and semiprecious stones. There were medals of brass, copper, silver and gold. Crosses came in all types: some plain and severe, some horrifyingly detailed, and others that could pass for fashionable jewelry.

Susan picked up a small marble statue of Michelangelo's Moses and handed it to a clerk, a nun dressed in white. Before she could get her money out, Michael took out his wallet and paid.

"Michael…" she protested.

"I insist. You're my guest in the Vatican."

They left and walked across the square. He wanted to ask where she was staying, if he could have dinner with her, but felt tongue-tied and anxious. They walked on in silence. She seemed unaware of his confusion.

As they reached the end of the square and stepped onto the street, Michael saw James leaning against an odd-looking little red car. With only a single seat for the driver, it resembled a large tricycle with an auto housing on top. It had one center front wheel and two normally spaced back wheels. James wore jeans, running shoes, and a T shirt that said *Save Souls, Not Soles.* It was too late to avoid him; James had seen them.

Michael greeted him with forced gaiety. "We can't seem to get enough of each other."

"I was just out for a run." James gave Michael a sidelong look. "Aren't you going to introduce me to your friend?"

"Susan Chambers," Michael said, feeling caught with his hand in the cookie jar. "She's a freelance writer from the United States. Susan, I'd like you to meet my very good friend, Father James Talman, S.J. M.B.A., Ph.D., Ph.D., Ph.D., and M.D."

Susan looked overwhelmed. "I'm not sure what all those initials mean, Father."

"Please call me Father James, or just James if you prefer." He gave Michael a wry look. "S.J. is for Society of Jesus. I'm a Jesuit priest. The M.B.A. is in finance. The Ph.Ds. are in theology, German, and psychology. I'm also a practicing psychiatrist."

Susan looked puzzled. "I thought you were a priest."

"I am, but Jesuits don't have parishes. We're free to practice a variety of professions."

"He left out that he's fluent in Latin, Romansch, German, and Chinese," Michael added.

"I think you two are having a little fun at my expense," Susan said skeptically. "You don't look like any priest I've ever met. And it would have taken a couple of lifetimes to do all that."

"I started in the Jesuit seminary when I was fourteen."

"You became a priest at *fourteen*?"

James smiled. "I didn't become a priest until I was in my twenties. The Society needs time to evaluate candidates, and many are rejected."

"I thought Catholics needed all the priests they could get."

That provoked a chuckle. "I suppose that's true, Miss Chambers. The rejects probably become Franciscans or Benedictines."

Michael laughed too, but Susan looked confused.

"So you learned all those languages in the seminary," Susan said, apparently undaunted.

"I learned Latin and German there," James said. "I spent my last two years of high school in Switzerland, where I learned Romansch and the Swiss German dialect. I studied Cantonese and Mandarin in college, and did two years of missionary work in China."

"Romansch," Susan said. "I've never heard of it. What language is that?"

"An ancient one. It's very similar to Latin, and is spoken by about one percent of the Swiss and Italian populations. It dates back to the Roman empire. I already spoke Latin, and I was in Switzerland anyway, so I thought why not."

"Sure." Susan tilted her head to one side, staring at James as if bemused. "Why not?"

"Are you Catholic, Susan?"

She shrugged. "I was baptized. But our family never went to church."

James smiled and nodded.

"I remember reading once that the Jesuits were sort of a special group of Catholics," Susan continued. "For a long time I thought they were a separate religion."

"The Jesuits are the intellectual elite of the Catholic Church," Michael said. "To get into Mensa, you need an IQ of about 130. The Jesuits wouldn't accept that kind of rabble. They only take the cream of the crop."

"Do all the Jesuits earn so many degrees?" Susan asked.

"We teach focus." James gave Michael a sharp glance. "We study every day and continue building and reinforcing our knowledge. I'm fifty-three years old. I started at fourteen. That adds up to almost forty years of focused energy. One can do a lot over that many years of concentrated effort."

"Think of it," Michael said with a grin, "a religious Rand Corporation. Thirty-one years of study alongside other dedicated intellectuals with IQ's in the stratosphere."

"Michael is no slouch himself." James grinned at him. "Ph.D. in finance from the University of Rochester, fluent in German and English, scion of one of the finest families in Italy. If only he had a sense of humor."

Susan smiled warmly at Michael and said nothing. Michael felt his stomach tighten again.

"Are you free for dinner tonight, Michael?" James asked abruptly.

"Yes."

"Good." To Michael's astonishment, James turned toward Susan. "Would you care to join us?"

She grinned. "Love to."

"Where are you staying? We'll pick you up at seven-thirty."

"The Lord Byron," Susan replied. "I'll see you then."

Michael watched as Susan hailed a cab and sped away. James said nothing, which surprised Michael as much as the unexpected invitation for both of them to dinner. He felt a little guilty at how eager he was to spend more time with her and turned to a more comfortable topic. "James, this effort by the Rota is going to take more than a few days. You have a practice in Chicago. You can't be traipsing all around the Vatican getting involved in this mess."

"I'll turn my practice over to a competent replacement."

His casual statement astounded Michael. James was committed to his work with hospital and clinic patients, had even risked serious injury for one of them. Michael couldn't believe James would turn his back on it. "You're walking away from everything you've worked for," he protested.

James shook his head. "*This* is everything I've worked for. We're finally going to clean house in the Church, and I'll need all the skills I've developed over the years to help."

Michael nodded, still not sure he understood.

"I'll pick you up at your apartment for dinner," James said. He turned and ran swiftly in the direction of the Tiber, a youthful figure in jeans with the face of an old wise man.

CHAPTER XII

Vatican City
Monday, June 17

"Here's the latest report, Father Miro." The young Franciscan friar held out a ream of beige papers.

Father Miro took the documents and gave a little grunt of satisfaction as he leafed through the pages. So far the Archangeli had $30 billion under management and the money was still pouring in. The Miro account was doing just fine, too. Of course, Miro was not his real name, but the alias was a precaution worth taking, and he could still get at the money.

The Archangeli had wised up over the years. They no longer took drug money or funds from other illegal activities. Criminals of that type were unrealistic about money, and they could be violent. The Archangeli had given back the cash belonging to the Ochoa family and Pablo Escobar Gaviria, the former heads of the Medellin drug cartel in Colombia. Now the Ochoas were in jail and Escobar was dead.

"Have we finally severed all ties with the Cali cartel?" Father Miro asked.

"Yes. We helped them spirit most of their money out of Colombia, but they know we no longer want their business."

"What about the Pepes and the northern Cauca Valley cartel?"

The friar nodded. "We've taken care of them, too."

"Good." Miro gave an inward smile of satisfaction. How easy it had been to take over this disorganized band, mainly Franciscans plus a mixed bag of Benedictines and Dominicans. He was the only Jesuit. Before he came to their rescue, their incompetence had nearly landed them in jail. Intelligent men, but they lacked discipline. They could thank their lucky stars that the Vatican would do almost anything to protect its own from scandal.

Before Father Miro saved them, in addition to laundering drug money, they had used Vatican bank deposits to curry favors with Italy's richest families and corporations. They granted loans that never came due, always granting another when interest payments on the first loan became a burden. The reverse Ponzi scheme blew up, because they looted the bank much faster than they took in deposits. Father Miro paid the right people to develop temporary blindness. It was better than Switzerland.

After taking over, he christened the group Archangeli—the Archangels. "We are the rebellious Archangels who would rather rule on earth than serve in the Vatican," he'd told the others. "We will use the power and influence of the Church to create unlimited wealth for ourselves." He knew what they didn't, that the real money wasn't in drugs or Ponzi schemes, but in tax evasion. With the U.S. government threatening to prosecute accountants who set up offshore tax shelters for wealthy U.S. clients, those clients were swarming to the Vatican Bank. The Archangeli set up offshore vehicles to hide cash and profits for a ten percent fee. A high price, but worth it to U.S. tax evaders if it put their money forever beyond the reach of the dreaded IRS. European business had picked up, too. Lichtenstein once was the haven of choice, but now the Archangeli were taking the lion's share.

"How are we doing in South America?" Miro asked the young friar.

"There's quite a bit of demand," the Franciscan said. "Some of these businesses started up with mysterious funding, but they're legitimate now, and they don't want to be taxed to death."

"Better than drug money," Father Miro said. "Tax evasion is a white collar crime, and these clients never threaten to kill anyone."

The Jesuits had pioneered profiting from moving other people's money, and Miro had learned well from them. The Archangeli now employed the tried-and-true techniques the Jesuits had used during and after World War II to help people make their money disappear from one country and reappear in another. No receipts, no traceable electronic trails, just an old-fashioned handshake. Once the money was out of the United States, Europe, and South America, the Archangeli deposited it in dummy accounts for their clients. Only then did the electronic fund transfers begin. Their database contained the account numbers, cross-reference names, and structure of the shell corporations meticulously outlined. No one suspected the Church. It was a masterful plan and solved their temporary cash shortfall.

He smiled as he thought about Milton's *Paradise Lost*. Lucifer, the fallen archangel, had his own kind of power and guts. Like him, Father Miro would rather rule the Archangeli than serve the Society if it came to that.

"Your Jesuit colleagues suspect us, though," the Franciscan went on with a worried frown. "But they're no better. They moved money for thousands of families over centuries. The Angelinis in Chile, the Romitos and the Valle family in Argentina..." He trailed off. Father Miro stared down at the papers in his hands, remembering.

The Valle incident in 1991 had been a valuable lesson for the Archangeli. They quarreled with the Jesuits in Argentina and kidnapped Francisco Valle's young son Mauricio, then demanded the Jesuits drop their threat to expose a drug money laundering scheme. Mauricio Valle was their insurance. Cowards all, the Jesuits caved in. Valle paid $6 million in ransom, and the Archangeli framed a few corrupt cops for the kidnapping. And Miro learned that violence was an effective weapon against the Society of Jesus. Unlike his fellow Jesuits, Miro enjoyed it.

Sanctimonious hypocrites, he thought. Agostino Romito was Mussolini's steel minister; his money reeked of corruption, as much as any client the Archangeli had since aided. *They would call me a traitor if they knew—but I am no different from them, except that they lack courage.*

Before long, Miro vowed, the Archangeli would be powerful enough to challenge the Jesuits on their own turf.

The Franciscan handed Father Miro another report. "This is what we lifted from the Jesuits' computers earlier today."

Father Miro opened it eagerly. As he reviewed the report, his face darkened. "That damned Mexican hedge fund," he muttered. "It's gone up by several billion." He knew the Jesuits managed some money for Emilio Loya, who owned most of Grupo Loya and controlled newspaper and magazine publishing and distribution throughout South America. In 2003, Loya's net worth was $5 billion, up from $3 billion a decade earlier. But that increase was nothing compared to what the Jesuits had done for him. In the past three years, with the help of Jesuit connections, Loya had undertaken buyouts and business partnerships throughout Latin

America that raised his net worth to more than $45 billion.

Loya now controlled every major Latin American publication outside of Cuba, Brazil and Nicaragua, and the Jesuits had earned more investment banking fees than a large Wall Street firm from Loya's business alone. Of course, the Jesuits called them advisory fees. And it was all perfectly legal!

"At least we can monitor their activity," the Franciscan said. "And our own ventures are doing well thanks to Father Pintozzi, God rest his soul." He bowed his head.

Father Miro gave him a disgusted look. Before Miro reined them in, the Archangeli had deluded themselves into believing they could predict the market. When they lost money on a trading position, they doubled their bets, hoping they would win, but they only accelerated their losses. Father Pintozzi had been invaluable, correcting mistakes and imposing discipline. Miro's staff had been both jealous and fearful of Matteo's skill. Matteo also helped them get information from Jesuit files to which even Father Miro didn't have access.

"When you live your life the way Matteo lived his, you bring things on yourself," the Franciscan said.

You are such a fool, Father Miro thought.

CHAPTER XIII

Rome
Monday, June 17

The view of Rome from the Pincio at night was the most spectacular in the city. The limousine pulled up onto a gravel parkway, and Susan, Michael and James alighted to see tables illuminated by small floodlights coming from the gardens in the nearby park. The *maître d'* escorted them to the best table in the restaurant, in the southwest corner of the terrace. To the east they could see the gardens; to the west, the western half of Rome.

Michael looked over at Susan. She wore a button-down blue silk dress gathered at the waist with a gold belt, and long earrings danced at her neck. She didn't appear to be wearing a bra, but then, she didn't need one.

Below them was the lighted Piazza del Popolo. A huge obelisk dominated the center of the piazza, similar to the one in St. Peter's Square. James saw Susan glance toward it. "The obelisk dates from the 13th century B.C. and was moved from the Circus Maximus, the ancient chariot race course made famous to Americans by the movie *Ben Hur*," he said.

"What about that huge marble gate at the piazza entrance?" she asked.

"Bernini designed it in the 1600s," he replied.

The eleventh-century chapel of Santa Maria del Popolo, said to be built over Nero's tomb, sat at the far side of the square. The lights from below seemed to bounce off the stone, and Michael could almost feel the excitement rising from the people in the piazza below. Further out, he could see the dome of Saint Peter's shining in the reflected light of the square below.

The day had cooled when the sun went down, and the evening air was heavy with a sweet fresh smell from the plants in the gardens. Fresh cut flowers and tall lit candles graced the table.

A waiter appeared, and James ordered. "We'll have white wine and antipasti, followed by fettuccine alfredo. Then whitefish sautéed in wine sauce, and grapefruit sorbet to clear the palate. After that, we'll have red wine with a roast veal chop, medium rare."

"Your usual wines, Father?"

"Yes."

Michael smiled at the exchange. James routinely phoned ahead to make sure restaurants stocked his favorite wines. They chatted pleasantly about Rome and its landmarks until the antipasti arrived, an assortment of prosciutto and marinated vegetables. Michael ate hungrily. It was his first full meal since breakfast.

Halfway through the rest of their dinner, Michael glanced at Susan and met her knowing smile. Suddenly he felt the soft leather of her sandal moving up the side of his leg. Then it stopped, and Susan briefly bent down. She sat upright again, and Michael felt her bare foot playing with the cloth of his pants. His own sense of pleasant arousal embarrassed him even as he enjoyed it. Susan's foot seemed to have a life of its own; he felt it sliding further up his leg and then moving in a slow half-circle around his inner upper right thigh.

"Michael," James said, "I'd like to show you something in a cathedral outside the city on Tuesday. It's stolen furniture, confiscated by the Society. I'll explain after you see it."

"Fine," Michael replied, struggling to keep his face impassive.

"Good. I'll fly us up in the Cessna. You might like to come along, Susan. You may get some ideas for your writing."

"Delighted," she answered with a bright smile. "So you're a pilot, Father James?"

He nodded and sipped his wine. "Just a skill I picked up along the way."

Susan's foot was still stroking Michael's leg. An awkward silence fell as Michael fought to keep his composure. "Stolen furniture," he said. "The Church seems to be involved in all kinds of illegal activities."

"Yes." Susan's eyes were wide and innocent as her foot gently brushed his crotch. "There certainly seems to be a lot of dealing under the table."

Michael let out a yelp that sounded halfway between an exclamation of surprise and laughter. Susan rubbed her bare foot against him, a gentle teasing pressure that made him hard. She stroked the length of his shaft with her foot. He was afraid to look at her, and looked at James instead. Susan likewise looked at James with an angelic expression on her face. Her lovely young, carefree face.

James gave her a wry glance. "It could seem that way. It only takes a few corrupt people in high places, without restraints on their behavior, to create a lot of havoc. You never know what they've got their foot into."

Susan blushed, and Michael felt her foot disappear. He gave a short, deep laugh and refilled her wine glass. "Would you like more wine, James?"

"No, thank you. I'll have some dessert, though."

They ordered chocolate gelato. The night breeze was pleasant but still very warm. As they finished eating, James broke the silence. "Would you care to join me in a quick drive around Rome?"

"Wouldn't miss it," Susan said with enthusiasm.

James had a car and driver waiting for them. Their first stop was the Colosseum, for a view of the ancient Roman gaming arena. The remnants of the towering structure spoke of the power and wealth of the dead civilization. Floodlights gave the ruins an eerie glow.

"Perhaps it's haunted by the ghosts of the tens of thousands of slaves and animals that died here to entertain a bored Rome," Susan said.

"I don't believe in ghosts," James said.

The next stop was the Piazza Venezia, where they visited the tomb of the unknown soldier and the Victor Emmanuel Monument. The huge white marble building, which Italians had dubbed the wedding cake, gleamed in the light that bathed the white stone. Back in the car, they turned in the opposite direction and headed across the Ponte Sant'Angelo. They drove between the white Bernini angels, bathed in the glow of spotlights from below. The lights around the Castel Sant'Angelo gleamed off the Tiber River, and the building created its own shadow in the water. Though no spotlight was trained on it, the dark angel atop the crypt was clearly visible. It seemed to soak up the light around it, like an ominous shadow.

They drove a few hundred more yards and stopped again. Lights shone on the Basilica of Saint Peter and the square surrounded by the flawless looking colonnade and statues.

"Rome is at her best at night, when the crowds thin," James remarked. "Buses cease spewing their choking fumes and the blare of honking horns dies away. No wonder the Romans take a siesta. The day holds no magic.

But when night falls, Rome is the most romantic city in the world."

"It's still early," Susan said. "Can we make one last stop at the Fountain of Trevi?"

They drove back to the fountain near the city's center. Japanese and German tourists were still there taking pictures, and ten year-old Roman night owls out with their families ate ice cream while staring at the shimmering water.

Susan made Michael toss coins over her shoulder as she snapped pictures with her camera. Even James joined in. They finally left when they ran out of coins.

As they dropped Susan off at the Lord Byron, Michael wanted to follow her in. He watched her dance up the stairs of the hotel, and briefly felt grateful for James as a chaperone.

"This trip wasn't entirely for pleasure," James said quietly. "I'd like to go over our hacker's data tonight."

***

The sound of gentle rapping made Father Jacques Pleurre look up in annoyance. Another intrusion on his few precious moments of peace since the discovery of Father Pintozzi's body two days ago.

The Rota had pushed its timetable ahead five years, and Father Pleurre had spent the last sixty hours talking on the phone, destroying the weekend plans of lawyers and bankers all over

Europe. The Latin Americans were coming tomorrow. He needed rest to be fresh for those meetings. "Come," he barked.

His irritation turned to pleasure when he saw James's head poke through the heavy oak door that opened into his study. "I'm not disturbing you?" James asked gently.

"Not at all," Father Pleurre replied with obvious pleasure. His smile turned to a frown as Michael Visconte followed James into the room.

"It's late," he said, looking at Michael.

James held up a thick folder. "We have some documents you need to see. It can't wait."

Father Pleurre hesitated, then took the folder. Inside lay a sheaf of papers. He started wading through them, then paused as he realized exactly what he was reading. Excitement spread through him, and he shook with nervous energy. He looked up at James, who frowned in concern.

"You've not eaten," James said. He reached over to a long braided bell cord and pulled it.

"Never mind that." Father Pleurre shuffled through the papers. "This is—"

A gentle rap came at the door, and a young deacon looked in. James ordered coffee and a late dinner for Father Pleurre. "Bring extra sandwiches along with the pasta, and some fruit and cookies. We have a long night ahead of us." As the deacon left, James turned to Father Pleurre. "Let's clear a space so we can work."

They moved Father Pleurre's clutter from the coffee table and shoved it all in the nearest bookcase, on top of a three-volume set of the *New Palgrave Dictionary of Money and Finance*. Then they set up a folding table for the food. Finally, Michael and James set out the papers James had brought. Father Pleurre noticed that they worked with the effortless coordination of long-time colleagues. He felt a pang of jealousy for their easy camaraderie.

Father Pleurre sat down, grabbed a handful of printouts and began poring over them. He felt like a soldier who'd found a hole in the enemy's defenses. The information Michael Visconte had stolen from the would-be intruder into the Jesuits' databases was at once a threat, a puzzle and an opportunity.

"Who is Father Miro?" Michael asked, from his seat across the table. "According to these files, he has transfer authority for all the accounts. That makes him the head of the Archangeli, more than likely."

"I don't know," Father Pleurre replied. "Let me check our clergy listings." He got up, went to his computer and printed out some names. He looked them over and frowned. "There are two of them: one in his nineties, in a Dominican retirement home, another a Jesuit running a mission in Africa. It's probably an alias."

"See what you can find out about them anyway," Michael said.

Father Pleurre glared at him. "If it's a false name, I don't see the point."

"Just to cover all the bases." He went on, in a respectful tone. "I would very much appreciate any information the Society can find. One never knows what might be useful."

Mollified, Father Pleurre reclaimed his seat and looked again at the computer output. Pure disdain at what he saw made him shake his head. "The Archangeli can't make a profit without resorting to tax fraud."

"By laundering money through offshore vehicles," Michael said with distaste.

"Look at the dummy corporations," Father Pleurre said. "They're headquartered here. It's outrageous. The Franciscans and Dominicans actually incorporated some of them in Vatican City. Very careless, when you consider how many alternatives they had to choose from."

"You need connections, though," Michael said.

Father Pleurre agreed. "The Archangeli were always impatient. No sense of continuity. If they had made friends in the lay community, they wouldn't need to muddy the name of the Vatican. They could have used Andorra, Monaco, Gibraltar, Liechtenstein, San Marino, the Isle of Man, the Channel Islands or a Caribbean tax shelter."

James set down a printout and picked up another. "I'm sure they tell themselves they're only managing the money, collecting fees. Just like the Swiss banks claimed when they accepted deposits the Nazis had looted from Jews. Or

Wachovia Bank, when it laundered Latin American drug money."

Father Pleurre grunted. "Back when the Society helped a few Jews escape with money, Vatican leaders too cowed to take a stand against the Nazis reprimanded us. Yet now the Vatican deals with tainted money, and no one says a word."

A knock at the door announced the deacon with their food: a platter of pasta with vegetables, several sandwiches on crusty rolls, assorted fruit and small cookies. Father Pleurre thanked him and sent him on his way, then turned to James. "Would you like something?"

"Not now," James replied. "We'll have some sandwiches later. Go ahead and eat; Michael and I will keep working."

Father Pleurre filled a plate, with a feeling of gratitude toward James. He'd been so caught up in work, he hadn't eaten all day. As he started on the pasta, he found himself savoring the taste. His inner tensions began to ease, and he allowed himself the luxury of getting lost in thought.

The Society was his life. As a young boy in Catholic France, he had felt isolated, constantly alone. People confused him. The affectations of upper-crust French society seemed boring, a waste of time. Most used social artifices as a device to hurt others. His own parents were no exception. An amiable, wealthy Frenchman, his father kept mistresses in the wings while dedicating himself to business, his real passion.

His mother, an impoverished Marquise, was happy enough with the arrangement. It gave her more time to manage Jacques, the object of her overweening ambition. She was determined he would marry into one of the many impoverished European noble families looking to sell prestige. Jacques would get no title, but the family star would rise all the same.

Jacques Pleurre, however, was never quite good enough for his mother. His social awkwardness annoyed her, and he became the target of constant verbal abuse. She mastered the subtle art of dissecting her victim: death by a thousand verbal cuts.

Even today, he sometimes heard the echo of her petulant voice: "Even a *child* should be able to conduct himself with more decorum than that; don't you even *care* about this family's future; *some* mothers would get upset if their son told them he wanted to study mathematics instead of the family business; if you *really* wanted to make your father happy, you would learn more about the defense industry; everyone understands why you don't have any friends."

He had escaped into schoolwork, and he lived in his mind. In France's Jesuit academies he found priests who shared his intellectual spark and encouraged its development. For the first time he felt visible, accepted, understood. He even formed a few cherished friendships among his newfound fellows.

The social life his mother engineered for him made his holidays a chore. The boys indulged in meaningless pursuits: gambling in Cap Ferret or buying sports cars. The girls were interested in the latest fashions and in the Pleurre family money. Their incessant posturing irritated him.

Jacques's decision to enter the Society saddened his father, though he didn't oppose the choice. His mother ranted and raved, and hit him for the first time in his life. She accused him of doing it just to hurt her: "If you *really* loved me, you wouldn't *want* to become a priest."

Years later, James told him the only possible response: "Of course I love you." But he didn't love her; he *hated* her. When she died he felt no sorrow, only empty anger and relief.

James Talman was his dearest friend, the only man he felt could truly trust. So different from Father de Aragon and Father Graf, the other two members of Father Pleurre's code group. Graf played the brilliant rogue and enjoyed infuriating him, while de Aragon was a slick diplomat. But James possessed rare gifts: he exuded goodness and it made him irresistible. People instinctively flocked to him for spiritual healing the way they flocked to warm springs to heal sore muscles. Over the years, Father Pleurre had come to admire James immensely, especially his radiant, powerful intelligence.

James taught Father Pleurre that verbal defense skills were like martial arts skills, though Father Pleurre never could master that. He felt uncomfortable with strangers and the verbal traps they set, and avoided outsiders. The Society served him as a womb, sheltering him from the general unpleasantness of the world.

He had repaid them by going into finance. He was mathematically gifted, and he loved it. Numbers didn't lie or hurt you, and for the most part they obeyed the rules. He became a wizard at making money. His work was his art, his creative outlet. He gladly undertook the daunting task of coordinating the Society's vast global wealth, hundreds of billions in cash, gold, real estate and artwork. He engineered a complex web of front corporations that earned fat investment fees and kept the Jesuits' wealth growing, though he made certain to keep things legal.

Through the Society, Father Pleurre acquired power and status. Top financiers around the globe feared him. On any given day, he could walk into the office of the president of any Swiss bank, knowing the bankers would stop what they were doing to meet with him. Likewise, the wealthy and powerful in Latin America and Europe always took his calls. But someone had put all that at risk. Someone had betrayed him, surely Father Graf or Father de Aragon. He desperately wanted to keep that power and status, and Michael Visconte had given him the means to make sure he could.

***

"Father Pleurre," Michael said. "Are you all right?"

"Yes, fine," Father Pleurre answered crisply. He had finished eating and his color looked healthier, but Michael thought he still seemed agitated.

Michael nudged a printout toward him. "Perhaps your Latin American friends can help us. A lot of this money is in Latin America. With the right connections, you could cook up an excuse to freeze the Archangeli's accounts."

Father Pleurre stared at Michael in frank amazement. Then he began to laugh, so hard his whole body shook. "That's beautiful," he exclaimed, wiping tears from his eyes. "It's perfect!"

Michael had expected a reaction, but nothing this effusive. Michael glanced at James, who merely shrugged. "Can you ask them?" Michael said.

"*We* can ask them," Father Pleurre responded. "The Latin Americans are coming to the Vatican. I'll set up a meeting for Wednesday. You can brief them and explain what is required."

"One more thing," Michael said. "You said Father Pintozzi prospered because of your invention. What did you mean?"

Father Pleurre gave a crooked grin. "*They* are my invention."

"The Latin Americans?"

He nodded. "They and others in Europe and the United States. They are our investors. We all help each other."

"How much money do you manage for them?" Michael asked.

"Currently, $150 billion. Nothing else we've ever done has brought in so much money, but we've only been doing it for six years, and we have a lot of expenses. Part of our fees subsidize our money-losing schools, other expenses of the Society and our missionary work."

An idea had begun to form in Michael's head. Hedge funds were limited to a hundred investors. All the investors in Father Pleurre's world were powerful, well-connected businessmen and bankers. Many of them had sons and daughters who wanted admission to good Jesuit colleges in the United States. If these investors handled the trading themselves, they would come under unwelcome scrutiny, and they didn't trust any individual to be the sole conduit of sensitive and valuable information. Having the Jesuits handle both was perfect. No one person among the influential investors had an unfair advantage over the others, but they all benefited.

The Jesuits used offshore funds and so paid no taxes on their hefty fees. With $150 billion in assets under management, the Jesuits were making $15 billion, tax free. Quite a war chest.

"It is all legal," Father Pleurre said. "Insider information is legal in some venues. That used to be true even in the United States. But we don't use insider information. Just very good information."

"George Orwell once said that the way to get rich is to start a religion," Michael said. "Orwell was talking about voluntary donations of money. But you're exploiting voluntary donations of timely and valuable information. That translates into more money than cash donations ever could."

Father Pleurre nodded, with a slight smile. "Yes. I see we understand each other."

Michael couldn't shake the feeling that Father Pleurre was holding back something important. Father Pleurre's lips smiled radiantly, but his steely eyes appraised Michael with cold disdain.

CHAPTER XIV

Vatican City
Tuesday, June 18

Father Pleurre woke up at 4:30 a.m. that morning, half an hour before his alarm clock would have done the job for him. He hadn't slept a full night for months. He got out of bed and did a short meditation, then the Jesuit examination of conscience and the Spiritual Exercises. Afterwards, he worked out and showered. By the time he finished, it was nearly six. He had a quick breakfast of whole-grain cereal with berries, orange juice and coffee. By 6:15 he was at work.

He sat in a chair surrounded by three large computer screens to his right, to his left and in front of him. His interactive phone lines sat by the computer on his left, within easy reach. Most days he took satisfaction in being surrounded by the tools of his trade. Today, fury gripped him—a feeling he hadn't experienced since he was a small child. He wanted revenge.

He had written a Trojan Horse program, a time-release virus that would destroy the Archangeli's software on Thursday. By then, their backup system would be contaminated, too. As he reached for his keyboard, he repeated the

Jesuits' motto silently to himself: *Ad majorem Dei gloriam.* For the greater glory of God.

He scanned the information and decided to do one last thing. This next step would put the Archangeli out of business for good. Father Pleurre entered the Archangeli's system one last time and typed in a few lines of code. Then he logged off.

A twinge of remorse nagged at him. Perhaps he had gone too far. As much as he wanted to feel sorry, though, he didn't. In truth, he was glad he had done it. Now more than ever.

***

At 7:00 a.m., James and Michael stood before double doors of dark oak adorned with carved vines. James knocked. A young Jesuit opened the door and looked out, then ushered them inside.

They stepped into a plushly carpeted room paneled in dark wood that was polished to a high luster. Thirteen chairs upholstered in leather surrounded the circular mahogany table in the center of the room. The Rota originally had twelve members. Nine of the chairs were already occupied. Michael and James took their seats. Of the two empty chairs that remained, one was for Father Zavala, who was escorting the Latin Americans. The second was out of respect for the memory of Father Mark Manion, who would never join them again.

Michael ran through his mental checklist from James's briefing as he nodded in greeting to the assembled priests. Seated at the table were Father Herzog and Father Heilman, who was also a member of Herzog's code group. Father Heilman's family owned Heilman Konzern, the German industrial insurance company. Father Fried was 71, a relative of the German Fried newspaper family. Father Bovier, 73, was a member of the French retailing family who wanted to expand into Italy. Next came Father Pleurre, whose family made defense aircraft; Father de Aragon, who claimed noble Spanish lineage; Father Greiner, 49, scion of Swiss conglomerate owners; and Father Aiello, youngest of the group at 47, who came from the famous Italian confectionery family. Father Zavala was from the family who controlled Banco Zavala in Spain; he was absent, still in transit. The Jesuits had amassed a following that included the representatives of influential military/industrial power throughout Europe and Latin America.

"Welcome," Father Herzog said. He signaled to the young Jesuit to leave, and waited until the door clicked shut behind him. Then he gave Michael and James a warm smile.

The group rose as a body and moved to the adjoining chapel, where the three oldest priests said a high requiem mass for Father Pintozzi. In unison, the Rota chanted aloud the words of the Communion, a prayer unchanged since the early Christians first chanted it in the catacombs: "*Haec commixtio et consecratio Corporis et Sanguinis Domini nostri Jesu Christi, fiat accipientibus nobis in vitam aeternam. Amen.*" Michael let the prayer wash over him while he pondered the enormity of what he was about to do, and the Rota could only accomplish its goal with his help. He thought of Helena and the boys. She had asked him to keep his distance from Father Pintozzi's death. He had said he would. Yet here he was. He could only pray he was doing the right thing.

After the mass, the Rota reassembled in the conference room. To Michael, the chamber felt alive with electricity. James had told him that the Jesuits originally planned to execute their operation around 2016, but the murders of Father Manion and Father Pintozzi forced them to act sooner. Just as well, Michael thought as he looked around the conference table. The financial pillaging and corruption of the Church, the deterioration of schools and moral crises in the parishes grew worse each year. Many Catholics in Europe and the United States were so alienated that it would be difficult to coax them back into the fold. Even Latin America was growing distant from the Church.

Michael drew in a deep breath. "May I present some new evidence to the Rota?"

"Against whom?" Father Herzog asked.

"Against the Archangeli. We can prove they have been managing funds for tax evaders."

Father Herzog nodded. Michael took a folder from the briefcase he'd left by his chair and distributed the contents: several copies of the relevant data files he'd stolen from the Archangeli hacker. "In these pages you'll find names, amounts, account numbers and records of meetings with tax-evading business clients. Giant bank deposits, phony transactions... it's all there."

A murmur went around the table as the Rota members absorbed the information in their hands. Father de Aragon glanced up. "Have you determined how much money the Archangeli manage for these tax evaders?"

Michael nodded. "Over $30 billion in a variety of accounts, mostly in Latin America, with some in the Caymans. They also have about $5 billion of their own money, earned in fees."

Father de Aragon glanced back down at the papers. "So who is Father Miro? And how did the Archangeli crack our system?"

Before Michael could answer, Father Pleurre gave Father de Aragon a hard look. "I'd feel a lot more comfortable if we knew the answer to that question. Do you have any ideas?"

The room fell silent. Father Herzog looked intently at Father Heilman and tapped the table with his fingers. The hush deepened. Father Herzog sat motionless, his concentration seemingly turned inward. The air in the chamber grew warmer and thicker.

Father Herzog gazed in turn at each of his subordinates. Father Heilman did the same. Michael thought he knew what they were looking for: the slightest muscle movement, the smallest flick of an eyelid or twitch of a mouth. He felt a subtle sense of pressure, as he had yesterday when Father Herzog first spoke with him. This time, though, the pressure was directed elsewhere. Father Herzog's troubled eyes came to rest on Fathers Pleurre and de Aragon.

"What are you hiding?" Father Herzog asked gently. "You feel guilty. Why?"

Father Pleurre didn't flinch. "I'm glad Visconte got the goods on the Archangeli. And I feel guilty our systems weren't impenetrable."

Father Herzog glanced again at Father Heilman. He tapped the table lightly, then sighed and turned to face the group. A cool breeze stirred the air and the room brightened. Michael took a deep breath, feeling as if a weight had just been lifted from his shoulders. Around him he noticed more than a few priests doing the same.

"God be with you over the next few days," Father Herzog said with a gentle smile. "We desperately need your help in this, the most critical time for the Society. Our prayers and blessings go with you." He sounded as serene as ever, but Michael could see Father Herzog was worried.

***

James came up to Michael as the meeting broke up. "Join me for dinner later, and afterwards we'll meet with Father Graf."

James didn't ask, Michael noted; he simply assumed Michael would make himself available. This was new for James, but a lot of things had changed about the man he had known in college. "Where would you like to have dinner?" he asked finally.

"Meet me at 8:30 in the Piazza Navona, at a restaurant called Ciampini. It used to be Mastrostefano. You may know it."

"I do. I'll see you there."

A young Jesuit appeared as if from nowhere to escort Michael off the grounds. He followed, still replaying the morning's events in his mind. The Rota now had fresh evidence of the Archangels' activities, in such detail that no one could ignore it. Not even a Pope who might not wish to see what was in front of his nose. Michael reached his car and drove to his office, feeling hopeful in spite of himself. Too many times over the past seven years he'd seen hope wither, when vital witnesses turned up dead or evidence of criminality that should have brought conviction didn't. But with the new evidence he'd garnered for them, the Jesuits might just be able to pull off their plan, and take over the Church without challenging the infallibility of the Pope.

It could work. If they managed to stay alive.

CHAPTER XV

Rome
Tuesday, June 18

When Michael brought them the stolen computer files and the Jesuits' accumulated evidence, the Specialists sprang into action. Years of frustration evaporated with the presentation of hard evidence against their nemeses, the Archangeli and their Mafia friends. Part of Michael's team flew to Milan; many of the men named by the Rota would be in that city, which was a financial center, a Mafia hub and the home of the defunct Banco Ambrosiano. Part of his team remained in Rome, also a financial hub. Two more of his men drove to Ostia to provide extra security at his villa.

Michael called Helena and told her things were moving quickly. The family should be able to go about their normal routine in a few days. He didn't know if this was true, but he wanted her to worry as little as possible.

Once all the arrangements were in place, he had just enough time to return to his apartment, work out, shower and take a cab to the Piazza Navona.

The sun was just beginning its descent as Michael stepped into the square. He entered from the southern end of the piazza at the fountain with the Moor and walked toward the Fountain of the Four Rivers in the center.

As always, the huge Baroque edifice acted like a magnet for the eyes. Bernini had designed it with a horse representing the Danube, a lion representing the Nile, some coins and an armadillo representing the River Plate, and a stream representing the Ganges. He had worked the papal emblem of keys and a crown into the design to symbolize the power of the papacy over the four continents of Europe, Africa, America and Asia. In the middle of the fountain was a pagan obelisk that had once been in the Circus Maximus. It was crowned with symbols from the Papal coat of arms: a dove and an olive branch.

Four jets of water cooled the air around the fountain. Michael felt the soothing breeze as he walked past. He saw James standing at the edge of the black iron railing that separated the outdoor tables of the Ciampini restaurant from the rest of the piazza.

Rudolfo, the *maître d'* nodded politely at Michael and then greeted James with effusive warmth, expressing genuine delight in his return to Rome. He ushered them to a large table with a direct view of the central fountain.

Umbrellas better suited to keeping out the sun than the rain towered over each table, held on their perches by shafts of smooth, blond wood. A gelateria made of wood and glittering brass stood next to the restaurant. Couples enjoying a lazy romantic summer night in Rome strolled past and occasionally stopped to buy gelato.

Michael and James exchanged pleasantries, and James ordered wine. They decided on salad, fettuccine for an appetizer and veal limone for an entree. The restaurant served veal that melted in the mouth with a silky smoothness, prepared the classic Italian way, which required long and careful pounding to break the fibers.

When they had finished ordering, James turned to Michael. "You look as if you want to ask me something."

Quite a bit, Michael thought, but he focused on the most immediate and practical matter. "When does Father Herzog meet with the Pope?"

"Friday. But we still don't know the identity of Father Miro, the leader of the Archangeli. We believe Miro is responsible for the murders of Father Manion and Father Pintozzi."

A beaming Rudolfo appeared with two plates in hand. "I took the liberty of changing your pasta order, Father. The one you ordered is merely average and the chef used too much garlic. This one is really special. Capellini with thin strips of chicken and capers in a light cream broth."

Rudolfo set the plates in front of them and sprinkled white truffle oil over the small mounds of pasta. Then he sprinkled fresh grated cheese in a perfect ring around the sides. He stepped back, clasped his hands and beamed at them again. "It is good to have you back, Father," he said, and then moved off to fuss over another pair of diners nearby.

As a member of Rome's distinguished old money elite, Michael was frequently courted in Roman restaurants, but Rudolfo lavished more attention on James than he had ever given Michael. The pasta was among the better dishes Michael had ever tasted.

The restaurant had filled up, and a line of hopeful newcomers waited for tables. The established Italian patrons were served the best food the chef had to offer. The restaurant also attracted an eclectic assortment of foreign tourists, but they were served more indifferent fare. The tourists never noticed any difference.

The waiters kept the tourists amused with jokes and flattery in the tourists' native languages, mainly French, German, Spanish and English. Only the Japanese baffled them. The waiters resorted to accented English, and the Japanese tourists smiled and nodded in polite incomprehension.

Michael's veal arrived, prepared with an excellence mere tourists would never enjoy. The waiter poured more wine and discreetly moved away.

"Tell me about this next meeting you've arranged for me," he said. "With Father Graf."

"You met him in the Vatican Museum when Matteo Pintozzi was killed. He's a medical doctor by training. He handles Society medical problems within the Vatican, but he is a multifaceted man."

"Is he a member of the Rota?"

"No." James paused, then added, "But Father Graf is a key figure in the Society administration."

"Was Father Pintozzi a member?"

"No. At thirty three, he was too young, but there were other reasons. Matteo was charming but impatient. He wanted everything fast and easy. Most recently, he was working closely with Father Pleurre to catalogue and appraise Jesuit-owned assets."

"And he was your mole?"

"Yes. He had an extraordinary way with people. He was a native Italian, and he was easily accepted among the people who formerly worked for Paul Marcinkus. Many of them were Italian. Perhaps, given more time..."

Rudolfo appeared again, and James fell silent. The waiter cleared their plates while Rudolfo hovered. "I have a special dessert in honor of your visit to Rome," he said, with visible pride. He plied them with fresh espresso and grappa, then swiveled as if wearing an invisible cape and disappeared.

The piazza had darkened, but the central fountain and the restaurant were well lighted. The beauty of the Piazza Navona at night captivated even native Romans. Small floodlights created sparkling rainbows in the mist of the fountain streams. The sound of the water blended with the voices of the people in the square to create an atmosphere of gentle exhilaration.

Michael thought of Susan and how much he would have liked to be with her right now. A young couple passed their table and kissed passionately about twenty feet away. They had the right idea, he thought. He spent his life steeped in murders and crime, missing the feeling of innocence the young pair seemed to enjoy.

He looked up to see James watching him intently. Michael shifted uncomfortably in his chair.

"All of you in the Rota seem to have a way of getting at people," he said. "It's unnerving. I must admit, I've never experienced anything quite like it before. It's as if you can read my mind."

James shrugged. "Just training."

A mild sense of shock prompted Michael's startled laugh. "The Jesuits train priests to read minds? If I weren't born in this century, I'd call it some sort of black magic. You shouldn't call yourselves the Rota; you should call yourselves the Necromancers."

James laughed. "You of all people should not be so quick to apply the term 'magic' to unfamiliar phenomena."

"I'm not, but when Father de Aragon spoke with me on Sunday..."

"Easily explained, if not easily practiced," James said. "Just as a gymnast can perform unusual feats with the body after years of practice, we can do the same with our minds. Unlike the gymnast, where youth is an advantage, age is our advantage. The brain grows more powerful with years of training and constant use."

"What sort of training?"

"We employ a variety of disciplines. We adopted ideas from Hindu fakirs for altering the physical environment to put the subject at ease, making him receptive to establishing a link. The techniques, which you call mind reading, are merely methods for establishing rapport. If you've ever seen a magician do mind-reading tricks, you know how amazing it can seem. But there's nothing mystical about them."

"You make it sound commonplace," Michael said. "In my work, we are taught how to make people open up to us, and how to tell when they're lying. But nothing like what you do."

James shrugged again. "There's a lot more to human communication than we can easily explain. Most of our communication is nonverbal, and most of our thoughts never find oral expression. Be assured, there is nothing supernatural about what we are doing."

Michael wasn't satisfied. James's answers were too slick, almost rehearsed. He had actually explained nothing.

"There's more to it than that. There was something very strange about Father de Aragon. Father Herzog was even stranger. They have a weird hold over people. I can't quite put a finger on it, but..."

"I think the word you're looking for is hypnotism," James said.

Michael stared at him. "*Hypnotism*?"

James laughed. "Have you forgotten your Jesuit lore? You've been missing a lot of obvious clues, and I have to say I'm disappointed in you. Quite a few strange things have been happening around you that you haven't figured out. I'm waiting for you to wake up."

Michael felt annoyed. "I'd like you to explain that."

"I'll explain the hypnotism, but some of it will have to wait until later. For now, do you recall learning about Father Gassner?"

It took a moment's thought, but then he remembered. "Yes, a little. But I thought that was a fable."

"No," James said firmly. "I'll refresh your memory. Father Gassner worked with Dr. Franz Mesmer and Father Hell, back in the late eighteenth century, and was credited as the true father of modern hypnotism. He was also a bit of a showman. He would enter a room holding a crucifix high in one hand and call out, 'Sleep' in a commanding voice, instantly creating a state of hypnosis in those present. He could have done it without the crucifix, but he couldn't resist a good performance."

Michael raised an eyebrow. "That was for real?"

"Yes. Hypnotism works very well on about eight percent of the population when performed properly. A much higher percentage of the population has somewhat lesser susceptibility. It's sometimes used more effectively than anesthetic to relieve pain. I use it in my practice. Father Gassner was a master, and we study his techniques. In his famous Lazarus experiments, he suspended his subject's heartbeat for several minutes, and then called the person back to life."

"So Jesus might have done the same thing..." Michael said slowly.

"Possibly," James agreed.

"So you're telling me that Father de Aragon's ability to make a room feel warm and Father Herzog's ability to get people to cooperate with him are merely magicians' tricks?"

James shook his head. "They're much more than that. They are the result of years of study combined with highly trained minds and uncommonly strong wills."

Sudden disgust swept through Michael. "I've had about enough of this," he said. "You seem to feel that you can manipulate people at will, without their consent."

James leaned toward him across their table. "We would never use this skill dishonorably." A long moment passed, and then James sat back.

From his face, he'd come to a decision. "I wonder what you think of us," he said quietly.

"What do you mean?"

"How do we appear to you? Are we a bizarre group of men, buried in their rarified Society, living in a world of the spirit and the mind with tenuous ties to the outside world?"

"You've done all right in the outside world," Michael said, easing back in his chair in turn. "Your psychiatric practice is very lucrative. Besides, why should you care what I think?"

"Because you are the Church," James said.

Michael gave a mirthless laugh. "My income and education bounce me out of the Everyman category, even if I'm not in the same class as your Latin American billionaire supporters."

James toyed with his coffee cup. "True enough. Nevertheless, the struggling masses make up the bulk of the Church, the people we were meant to serve. Perhaps the Jesuits, by elevating themselves above the mundane concerns of life, are out of touch. We must reconnect with the masses, or the Church will die. The Society is even willing to make overtures to the women of the Church."

"The women?"

"Yes. We don't advertise it, but when the Jesuits were formed, St. Ignatius made a conscious decision to exclude women. It's ironic, since he accepted financial support from many noblewomen."

Michael smiled at that. "Including Giovanna de Aragon, my ancestor."

"Yes."

"Yet he wouldn't admit women into the Society." Michael thought about that. The Church was about to be taken over by a group of Jesuits, whose founder had no use for women. He felt suddenly sad as he remembered Irena, recalling the horrible consequences of such attitudes throughout the Church.

"He wasn't a misogynist," James said gently.

"Mind reading again?"

"I don't have to be a mind reader to know what you're thinking. St. Ignatius felt the Society could not deal with the special problems posed by women. But he didn't hate them, or disdain them."

"My wife wouldn't enjoy hearing that the Church thinks she poses special problems." Michael paused. "Was St. Ignatius a homosexual?"

"He was as far in the other direction as one can get," James said. "Before he founded the Society, he was the quintessential seducer. He even killed a man in a duel over a woman."

"I vaguely remember that. But if he was so enamored with women, why did he become a priest?"

"Father Meissner explained it in his book, *Ignatius of Loyola, The Psychology of a Saint*. It's a psychobiography born of his work as a clinician and a prominent psychoanalytic theoretician."

"A *psychobiography*. It figures a Jesuit would make it into a cerebral exercise."

James laughed. "Well, it took a psychoanalyst to make sense of Ignatius' motivation. He was born to a noble Spanish family and aspired to become the paragon of hidalgos: a soldier, courtier and seducer. He exhibited all of the symptoms of a phallic narcissist characterized by exhibitionism, self-aggrandizement, arrogance, unwillingness to accept defeat and a need for power and prestige. That was before his crippling injury."

"He limped, didn't he?" Michael remembered that St. Ignatius had been maimed.

James nodded. "Meissner held that if Ignatius' leg hadn't been shattered by a cannon ball in battle, he would never have become a religious leader. At first he didn't accept his condition. He had his leg broken and stretched more than once in an attempt to straighten it and restore his former physical form. But he remained disfigured with a pronounced limp for life. His days as a seducer were over, and he could no longer soldier for a career."

"But why as a priest? That seems a huge leap from life at court."

"Ignatius had to build a new life. His motivation to become a priest probably stemmed from his infirmity: spiritual ambition replaced his social ambition. He could no longer seduce women, so they had to play a new role in his life. He employed his old charm to a new end.

He became close to Princess Juana of Spain, the daughter of the Emperor who became regent of Spain. Princess Juana pressured St. Ignatius into making her a temporary member of the Society. She was the only woman who even got that close again, only because Ignatius couldn't refuse her. He required her influence and financial support."

"So he still used women, but this time for their money," Michael said.

James sighed. "The Society will not change. Women do not have a role as priests, and that will not change either."

"So you'll take on the Pope, but you won't address the inequity toward women. I think that's a mistake."

Rudolfo arrived with their desserts, along with exaggerated apologies for the delay. He had prepared two plates with chocolate truffle paté, raspberries soaked in brandy with crème Anglais on the side, a small piece of tiramisu and assorted biscotti. He set two more glasses of grappa next to the deserts. Michael sampled each dessert, but noticed that James touched none of the sweets or the alcohol. In fact, James had drunk only a couple of sips of wine all evening. Thinking back, Michael realized that James had barely touched his champagne or his wine the previous evening.

"You've given up drinking," Michael said in surprise.

"Yes. The Society is very health-conscious these days. There are so few younger men. More than that, alcohol and other indulgences interfere with our mental processes, and we need clear heads. Especially now."

It dawned on Michael that the "special dessert" had been ordered in deference to his tastes. The entire dinner had been planned to make him feel more comfortable, more disposed to help the Rota. He wavered for a moment between renewed annoyance and sympathy. Were the Jesuits that uncertain of him, or that desperate?

"You don't have to entertain me, old friend," he said. "I am committed to this investigation." Helena would object if she knew, and he thought uneasily of her and the boys... but he was in it now, and he had to see it through.

"It's been a long time," James answered. "I've changed; you've changed. The Society is changing. The Society needs friends like you, Michael. Resourceful people, committed people, intelligent people. We want to get closer to you. Perhaps when this is over, you will want to get closer to us, too."

Michael said nothing.

James looked across the piazza and nodded toward the Baroque façade of the Church of Saint Agnese in Agone. "That's where we're going," he said.

The building was dark. "Father Graf is waiting for us in the church?"

"No, in the building next to it. Look up and to your right."

Michael looked across the piazza. He saw a lighted window on an upper floor of the building next to the church. A rectory, perhaps.

They paid the bill and Rudolfo hurried over. He clasped James's hands, asked them both to come again soon, and fussed over them until they exited through the gate.

***

Out of the warm yellow glow from the restaurant, the piazza seemed darker and more sinister. Michael saw it through a policeman's eyes, a hotbed of petty theft and the commonplace rip-offs of Roman street life. In one corner of the piazza, a man sold marijuana. In another, an artist selling ink drawings reassured a German woman that his work was at rock bottom prices and also on display in a Toronto art museum. Her husband stood at her side, arms folded as if skeptical. He said nothing as his wife pulled out a wad of euros and paid three times what every other street vendor was charging.

Well-dressed gigolos circled around lone females in the piazza like many sharks smelling blood in the water. The gigolos all spoke several languages with varying degrees of competence. Michael didn't have to hear their conversations to know how this game went. A gigolo would flatter a woman, ask where she was staying, how long she would be in Rome and if she had friends or family in the city. When her departure date neared, he would ask her to dinner at a restaurant, where he knew the waiters and didn't have to pay. Before his victim knew what was happening, he would be gone, along with her purse, her passport, her money and her credit cards. It worked because intelligent, educated, worldly women took risks on vacation they would never take at home. They all had the same surprised reaction: "But he seemed so well dressed, so educated, so nice."

On the far side of the piazza he saw a gang of local Italian boys shaking down a young Chinese woman selling cheap Asian jewelry. They wanted protection money for the right to sell her wares. They pushed her down and scattered her boxes of souvenirs on the ground. Michael tensed, then relaxed as a vigilo rushed to the scene. Minor skirmishes like that happened every day. The Chinese were becoming a larger minority in Italy. In a year or so, they would have their own little Mafia to add to the colorful street scene.

Most of the tourists milling around the piazza were unaware of anything but the beautiful Roman night. But for Michael, the romance of the night had disappeared. Sometimes Rome was like a woman with beautiful hair, but when you ran your fingers through it, a wig came off in your hands, exposing her bald head.

· Helena had chased this feeling out of his life years ago. He'd thought it was behind him, but now he knew that it never would be as long as he stayed a cop. He felt suddenly empty and thought of Susan.

***

At the rectory, James rang a bell recessed in the carved wooden door post. A buzzer sounded, and he pushed the door open.

Ahead of them, soft yellow light illuminated wide stone stairs. Next to the stairs was an antiquated brass-gated elevator whose smooth gleam showed frequent polishing. They walked up three flights. As they reached the third floor landing, another large wooden door down the hall swung open and a manservant gestured for them to come in.

Michael glanced into the dining room, where a table was set for two with fine bone china plates and handcrafted silver. Crystal goblets, a large one for water and two smaller ones for red and white wine, stood ready at each chair. A savory smell of garlic and tomatoes wafted through the air. He noticed a silver coffee service on an antique sideboard and a large Oriental rug patterned on a field of intense blue that provided the only splash of color in the room. The effect was one of elegance, refined taste and old money.

Father Graf was obviously expecting someone, and Michael guessed that someone was female. This must be Father Graf's cozy little pièd-a-terre, his seduction chamber.

The manservant showed them through the next door to the left, where Father Graf waited for them in a comfortable study. He wore an Armani suit that flattered his muscular frame. He stood to greet them, and Michael saw a wary look in his eyes.

"Welcome to my little retreat," Father Graf said. "I've had my man prepare coffee and cognac. If you like, I have cigars as well."

Michael shook his hand and thanked him. "I'll accept the coffee, but pass on the cigars and cognac, if you don't mind."

Father Graf had a strong grip; the bulge of his muscles as he pumped Michael's arm suggested he worked with weights. He was the same age as James, but the two men couldn't have been more different. "Rolf Graf," he said, sounding terse. "It's good to see you again, Mr. Visconte." His frozen grin belied his words.

Graf turned away from Michael, and his expression warmed. "James, you're back! It's been too long." He spoke with genuine pleasure. "You're looking very well."

James smiled back with equal warmth. "It's good to see you too, Rolf."

Father Graf held a chair for James, and abruptly gestured for Michael to sit down as well. He exuded the brash assurance of a jet-setting tycoon who believes money can open almost any door and is willing to trample anyone in his path who doesn't join him or get out of the way.

The valet came in with the silver coffee service, set it down on a nearby table and then walked out, silently closing the door behind him.

They sat, and James began speaking. "Father Graf performed the autopsy on Father Manion."

"Autopsy," Michael said, surprised. "Where was it performed?"

"In the Vatican. We have a small medical facility there," Father Graf said as he poured himself coffee.

"You had proof he was murdered, and you didn't turn the body over to the Roman police?"

James interrupted, with an intensity that startled Michael. "He was a Jesuit, and it happened in the Vatican. Father Manion was my friend. Someone outside the Society brutally murdered him. The Society was not about to abandon him, not even in death."

Father Graf looked upset by James's outburst. Uncomfortable, almost ashamed.

"I'm sorry," Michael said. "I spoke out of turn, James, and I'm sorry for your loss." He waited a moment before continuing. "What was the result of the autopsy, Father Graf?"

"Father Manion died of an epidural hematoma," Father Graf said softly.

"Could you give me more details?"

"Certainly. Father Manion suffered a skull fracture. A torn artery leaked blood inside the brain. The pressure of the blood on his brain killed him."

"Would he have died instantly?"

"No. It takes time to build up pressure."

"Then there would have been symptoms."

"Yes," Father Graf said. "Confusion, incoherence, drowsiness, possibly nausea."

That fit, Michael thought. The vigilo's report described exactly those reactions. Father Manion had been hit over the head and probably lost consciousness. He must have woken and wandered off, surprising the hell out of his murderers.

"Where is the body now?" Michael asked. "We need it as evidence."

"We buried it," Graf said.

"You buried it?"

"Yes. We decided to handle the matter ourselves; Vatican security didn't know about the murder. After the autopsy, I performed the last rites. Father Manion was an orphan, so there was no one to inform."

"What about Father Pintozzi? Did you perform an autopsy on him, too?"

"Yes. His neck had been sliced through, probably with a sharp wire. He died of blood loss from a severed artery. It must have been quick."

James stirred in his chair. "Poor Matteo," he said sadly.

"Do you still have Father Pintozzi's body?" Michael asked.

Father Graf nodded. "It's in cold storage under Vatican guard. No one can get close to it without special permission from the Superior General."

Michael eyed Father Graf in silence. He was hiding something. Perhaps he was under orders from the Rota not to say more. Or perhaps it was more than that.

"Well, thank you for your time," Michael said finally. "I have no more questions." Somehow, he didn't want to linger for the promised coffee.

As they left the study, Michael smelled a trace of familiar perfume and saw a light on under the closed right-hand door. Probably a bedroom. Father Graf's next visitor had arrived.

As if he had guessed Michael's thoughts, Father Graf looked straight at him, prepared for anything he might say. Michael merely nodded good-night and opened the door to the hallway.

Father Graf shrugged, like a schoolboy caught in a prank. "Please let me know if I can be of any more assistance in your investigation."

Neither Michael nor James spoke until they were out in the piazza.

"You suspect him, don't you?" Michael asked. Michael thought Graf was so arrogant that he didn't care that his insincerity was transparent.

"Yes. He has the right personality profile, the means and the opportunity. I wanted your impression, though, because some things just don't add up."

"Such as?" Michael asked.

"If he were our betrayer, he would have ordered Matteo's murder. The Archangeli may have discovered Matteo was our spy, but I don't see how. We allowed Matteo to cooperate and give them valuable information and passwords to earn their trust. Father Graf was having breakfast with me when Matteo was murdered. He was with me when he got the call from the guards, and he was genuinely upset. Shocked as well."

"It could have been an act."

"Maybe. But I know Rolf Graf well. He was definitely disturbed by the news."

Michael reflected on what James had said. He didn't like Father Graf, but that didn't make the man an embezzler and a killer. Father de Aragon had impressed Michael, despite his distaste for the man's sexual preferences. But Michael's admiring him didn't make him innocent. Father Pleurre, the third of their potential suspects, was a difficult man to like. He was cold and a bit hostile, but his off-putting manner seemed to stem from his deep need to protect the Society. Still, Michael admitted, the man was difficult to read, and his seemingly fierce loyalty to the Society could be a performance.

None of the three men had known of Matteo Pintozzi's role as a spy for the Society, and none was aware that he had passed on sensitive information as a ruse to gain the Archangels' trust. No, Michael corrected himself, that wasn't quite true. The Society's traitor might have been the recipient of Matteo's bait, and might have doubted Matteo's loyalty. Still, that was a reason to keep Matteo alive, not to kill him. A double agent could be used to the traitor's advantage so long as he didn't know the Archangeli were on to his game.

***

Michael sat for half an hour in his car, parked in the rotunda at the base of the sweeping staircase that led to the entrance door of the Lord Byron Hotel. He wanted to talk to Susan. He knew she had issued an implied invitation, but could he live with himself if he did this? He glanced at the passenger seat, at the bouquet of orchids he'd bought, and asked himself what the hell he thought he was doing.

He wanted to ask Susan a few questions. Hadn't he seen her in the crowd at the Vatican Museum the morning Father Pintozzi was murdered? She'd had reddish hair, he was sure. Why did she bleach it? If she was at the museum, why had she never asked him about the murder?

It sounded crazy, the more he thought about it. Perhaps he was mistaken. Yet he couldn't shake his doubts, or his desire. He wrestled with both for a few more minutes. Finally he made his decision, got out of the car and walked up the steps.

He knocked gently on Susan's door. She opened it as if expecting him, and Michael extended an armful of orchids.

"You are a dinosaur," Susan said, looking at the orchids. "I expected you last night, but better late than never."

She crossed to her dressing table and put down the flowers, unable to hide her smile of pleasure. Her casual manner disconcerted Michael. There was so much he wanted to know about her. But was that wise? He was married and she was obviously too willing. He had made a mistake, and was half prepared to leave. She turned and gave him a speculative look, then walked back over to him.

"I'm glad you came." She moved to face him and brushed his hair off his forehead with her hand. She put her arms around him, and he bent to kiss her.

He was excited and nervous, as if it were his first time. But he wanted to take this slowly, have a drink and talk a little. He had imagined them touching each other, as if by accident. He wanted to build up to this as if the depth of their attraction surprised them, as if making love had been unplanned.

Susan unbuttoned her blouse. Her gestures seemed matter-of-fact. She quickly removed her blouse and brassiere, while Michael mutely watched her. She reached for his hand and drew it towards her naked breasts.

"Don't," he said unsteadily. "I just came to drop off the flowers." He turned and stumbled roughly against an end table before reaching the door to her room. He didn't trust himself to turn around as he left. He fled the Lord Byron, unsure who he'd surprised more: himself or Susan.

As soon as he got back to his car, he picked up the car phone and called Helena. She answered in a voice filled with sleep.

"I'm coming back to the villa tonight," he said.

"You woke me up to tell me that?" she answered, a sudden smile in her voice.

"I was hoping you were still awake." He felt a twinge of embarrassment. He also felt like a fraud, something he had never felt before when he talked to Helena.

He wasn't sure why he needed to see her so urgently, but it was enough for now that Helena would be waiting for him.

***

Helena closed the door and walked swiftly over to Michael. She drew his head down to hers and kissed him roughly and fully on the mouth. The tension the past few days and Michael's absence had created a feral hunger. Michael hugged her and lifted her up so that her feet barely touched the ground. She sighed and rubbed her hips against his loins in a gentle, undulating motion. She slipped her right thigh up to his hips and pressed against him, kissing him deeply, then moved her mouth softly down his neck and gently sucked at the sensitive skin.

She wore no stockings, and her legs were smooth and bare. He could feel her heat through the thin silk of her dress. Her perfume was heady, combined with the musky aroma of arousal.

Michael was so hard that he pushed her away a little, afraid that he might explode right then. Helena gave a little growl of protest, but he held her hips away from his and let her feet touch the floor. She pushed him towards the bed and then down. She pressed her mouth against his and slid her hands over his torso, quickly unbuttoning his shirt and pushing the cloth aside to expose his bare chest.

Next she slipped her panties down and kicked them away with her sandaled feet. She reached down and slowly removed her sandals, leaning her body against his. She unbuttoned her dress, and he saw that her nipples were hard.

She kissed him again, more deeply now, and pressed her firm, rounded breasts against him as she undid his belt buckle. It took all his willpower to keep from coming while her hands fluttered at his zipper, touching him, stroking him, maddening him.

She moved a little away to let him calm down a bit, but kept her lips pressed to his. Her tongue sought his, flicking in, flicking out. She moved her mouth down his chest and hovered briefly above the area he most wanted her to touch. Then she shifted downward, running her lips over his thighs, over his testicles, and back to his thighs again while her hands caressed his stomach.

Suddenly she took him in her mouth, sucking him, flicking her tongue against the head of his penis, then sucking again. He tried to raise her up to him, but she laughed softly and pushed him down. She took him to the point of orgasm, then stopped and stroked him lightly, letting him calm down a little again.

He thought he was back in control, but she mounted him, riding him. She was wet and hot, and he slid easily in and out while her inner muscles caressed his cock. She bent down and kissed his mouth, moving her hips up and down against him. Her hair brushed the side of his face. She controlled the rhythm and the pace, and she used her hands to control his movements beneath her.

Michael tried to wait, but he couldn't anymore. He came in hot powerful bursts, writhing with loud moans.

Gradually, he came back to conscious awareness. Helena held his head in her hands and kissed him. She looked into his eyes and smiled, a feline expression of triumph. "Feeling better, Mr. Visconte?"

"Never better, Helena." He had nearly said *Irena*, and for a moment panic gripped him. He didn't want her to notice; he pulled her close and kissed her long and deeply on the mouth.

"Good. That was for you," Helena said. "Rest while you can, because the next one is for me."

Michael held her in his arms while she nestled against his chest. He was glad she couldn't see his face. He was wide awake. The sex had taken care of his physical need, but it hadn't brought him peace of mind. He didn't know if his urgency was for Susan or if he had been reaching back for Irena when he went to Susan's room. He had the uncomfortable feeling that he had just used Helena, something he had never done to his wife before.

CHAPTER XVI

Rome
Wednesday, June 19

As soon as he awoke, Michael phoned his answering machine in Rome for messages. One from James said he would meet Michael and Susan for breakfast at the Lord Byron at nine, where they would pick up Susan for the trip outside of Rome.

The drive from Ostia took just over half an hour. James was waiting in the dining room when Michael arrived, virtually on Susan's heels. Susan gave Michael an amused look, as if she sensed his consternation. Whether James noticed anything, Michael couldn't tell.

The Lord Byron's restaurant had a cheerful intimacy: the colors were light, the room airy. Soft white tablecloths and polished silver adorned the tables, and the chairs had bright-colored plush cushions that one could sink into after a long night on the town.

A waiter appeared with pots of strong, aromatic coffee. As he drank, Michael thought there was nothing better in the morning than fresh coffee in Rome. He tried not to think about the fact that he was having breakfast with Susan after thinking of her while making love to his wife.

They helped themselves from a buffet of croissants, rolls, cereals, fruits, yogurts and juices. Within twenty minutes they were finished and went out to James's car, a cream-colored Rolls Royce Corniche III. James whisked past the morning traffic to Ciampino airport, where the Society parked its private planes.

James helped Susan climb into the twin-engine Cessna and stow her shoulder bag, and then performed his preflight check. Fifteen minutes later, they were soaring towards the clear blue skies over Rome.

The flight from Rome to their destination took just over an hour. Michael spent most of his time looking out the window at the passing landscape. Flying below the clouds, they had a clear view of the suburbs of Rome, then some smaller towns and finally the bucolic countryside. James landed on a private airstrip somewhere north of Rome and south of Assisi.

The landing strip only had a few hangars and was used by some of the local landed gentry. They left the plane tucked inside a small but solidly constructed shelter out of sight from the road, then went outside to where a young man waited by a car. They drove twenty minutes or so past some farms. The only signs of life were a couple of cars on the back roads and few penned animals.

Their car finally rolled to a stop in front of a large cathedral. The grounds surrounding the old church were overgrown with weeds, and the stonework looked eroded by weather.

"This building is certainly an antique," Susan said as they got out.

"What's this all about?" Michael asked.

"That should be clear once we're inside," James said. He bounded up the stone stairs to the doors of the church and produced a large metal key from his cassock. He unlocked the massive doors and swung them open. No sound from their hinges, Michael noted; someone took care to keep them well-oiled.

Devoid of pews and statues, the ancient church looked like a warehouse full of antique furniture. Michael recognized some of them: Louis XIV, Biedermeyer, Queen Anne, even some antique Chinese pieces. There were armoires, headboards, desks, humidors, clothes chests and small tables.

Susan wandered around, gazing wide-eyed at the collection. Michael walked over to a cluster of Louis XIV desks and ran his hands over the wood, evaluating and appraising each piece. "Who owns all this?"

"The Society. It's all for sale."

"But—" Michael subsided abruptly as a thought struck him. "Do you have any tools here?"

James's face revealed nothing. "There must be some around here somewhere." He glanced around, then walked over to a corner and returned with a well-equipped tool chest. Michael took it and scanned the crowded chamber, then chose a Queen Anne chair upholstered with a delicate flowered needlepoint.

He took a large screwdriver from the chest. "May I?"

James waved a hand. "Be my guest."

Michael flipped the chair on its back and removed the cloth covering under the seat cushion. With a few deft strokes he pried the seat off. He ran his hand over its back and inspected it carefully. The upholstery tacks were expertly fastened, but he saw no other marks on the seat. No trace of earlier tacks removed during re-upholstering, as should be expected for an antique chair.

James smiled down at Michael. "Well?"

"They're good," Michael said. "They're very good."

"You mean in good condition," Susan said. She had come up to him while he worked, standing close enough to hint at intimacy. Michael flicked a glance at James, but the priest made no comment.

"No," Michael said. "They are very good reproductions. I can't be sure without looking at each piece, of course, but I think they're all very good fakes. The wood has been stressed to make the furniture look old, but these pieces were made recently."

Susan looked shocked. "I certainly couldn't tell!"

James kept silent. Michael rose to his full height and addressed him. "You knew they were fakes," he said.

"Yes."

"Did you think I'd be fooled?" Michael asked with indignation.

James grinned. "No."

Michael's next words came out with an edge. "So what is the Society planning to do with this stuff? Sell it to gullible buyers?"

To his amazement, James started laughing. It took him several seconds to regain control. "Of all the reactions I expected," he said, "that was not among them."

"Then what is this all about?" Michael asked.

"The Society does want to sell this furniture. But not as antiques. We want to sell them for exactly what they are, very good reproductions. I understand there's a good market for this kind of thing."

Relieved, Michael chuckled. "Sorry. All the chicanery lately has got me seeing bogeymen in dark corners."

"You're not far off the mark. The Society confiscated this furniture from a gang that was trying to do exactly what you feared, defraud unsuspecting buyers."

Michael looked at the furniture and shook his head with admiration. "This really is good work." He paused and ran his hands over a chair. "I'll eventually find the men who made this. We could do a healthy legitimate business with them."

James nodded. "But the furniture is the least of it." He led them toward a heavy velvet curtain near one side of the chamber and pushed it aside. Michael gasped. Behind it were piles of antique silver platters, stacked from floor to ceiling.

"Sevso silver!" Michael said.

James shook his head. "Not exactly."

Susan stared at the glittering towers. "What is Sevso silver?"

"Fifth century Roman silver," Michael explained. "It's called Sevso because of an inscription on the platters, and it is very valuable."

"Except this isn't genuine Sevso silver," James said. "Father Pintozzi couldn't verify its authenticity with a visual check, so he ran a few tests. These pieces are fakes."

"The silver looks real to me," Susan said.

"Oh, it is," James said. "The silver alone is quite valuable. The metal's price is skyrocketing, and the workmanship adds even more value. But they aren't fifth century Roman silver. They're masterfully done copies."

Michael swept his gaze over the cathedral space. "I'll have someone from the department come back and take inventory. We'll need a team. This is a lot."

"Already done," James said. "We have pictures and measurements to go with the list."

"This will make a great story," Susan said. She rummaged in her shoulder bag and pulled out a small camera. "Do you mind if I take a few pictures?"

"Go ahead," James said. "I've had photos taken, and you're free to use them as well."

"I don't know how to thank you," she said.

"Just write a good story. I've made arrangements for you to stay at Michael's villa in Ostia. Helena is expecting you. Much more beautiful and quiet than the Lord Byron. A perfect place to write. Don't you agree, Michael?"

Michael couldn't answer. The earth seemed to tilt slightly, and the blood roared in his ears. Something was going on here that he didn't understand, but he could read nothing in James's angelic expression. His stomach turned over, and he prayed Susan would turn down the invitation.

Susan grinned. "Great idea. "I'll have my things packed in no time."

James nodded with satisfaction. "When we get back to Rome, I'll drop you off at the Lord Byron. Michael and I have some business to take care of at the Vatican. After we're finished, we'll swing by and pick you up. We'll all have dinner at the villa."

Michael forced a weak smile.

CHAPTER XVII

Vatican City
Wednesday, June 19

Father Rolf Graf sat as if he had just turned to stone. He could not believe what he was hearing. He had expected they might oust him from the top administration, but they couldn't kick him out of the Society. They didn't have the authority. And it wasn't just the Society. They threatened to defrock him, to kick him out of the priesthood.

He looked around the familiar Jesuit study, with its polished wood paneling, heavy antique furnishings and Persian carpets. He wanted to look anywhere but at the three priests sitting across from him. He felt warm and knew his face was flushed. Stupid, to show any loss of control like that.

It was all so impossible, so outrageous. He had no warning. They must have been planning this, plotting against him for a very long time. Just the three of them. Or at least Herzog and Heilman. They had always hated him; they wanted to hold him back.

"You can't do this," he growled. "The others won't go along with it."

"We are all in agreement," Father Herzog said. "This is not just our decision; this is the decision of the Rota."

Graf scoffed. "It won't stick. Some priests will never go along with your forcing me out. James, you support me in this, don't you?"

He was shocked when Father James shook his head.

"No," James said. His tone was gentle, and his eyes showed regret. "I don't. I advocated for this action. You cannot break your vow of celibacy and remain a Jesuit, let alone a priest. You must choose."

Graf sagged in his chair. He was willing to fight these two old men, but James was too much. James hadn't sponsored this, he couldn't have. They were lying. They had pressured James. James was a priest for modern times, he would never go along with sending the Society back to the dark ages.

He appealed to James directly. "You would do this to me. You, of all people. I was your mentor. You know I don't deserve this." His lip curled in a sneer. "It's not as if I've slept with little boys. I prefer women, and the women don't seem to mind. I've been discreet as well. Where is the harm?"

"You took a vow," James said. "The values of the Church have to mean something, or there's no reason for us to exist. You knew that once. Or I thought you did."

Father Herzog intervened, his clear gray eyes boring into Graf's. "You can talk to the others if you like. You will find we are all of one mind on this issue."

Graf looked at the three priests calmly sitting before him. He wanted to rail at them, to shatter their collective composure.

"Von Herzog the Father General, Heilman the Son, and James the Holy Ghost," he spat. "The three of you sit there playing God. The grand patriarch, the dutiful son doing his father's bidding. And you, James, the unfathomable specter."

"We are not playing at anything. We are only asking you to comply with the solemn vows you took. It is your choice."

"You want me out," Graf snapped. "You don't think I'm good enough. You think you're so superior, so holy, so worthy. But I know better." He leaned forward and lowered his voice. "None of us are innocents here. I broke the celibacy rule, but there are worse things." He glanced at Father Heilman. "I'm sure you agree, Father. And I'm sure we can *all* agree that certain matters are best left alone."

Father Heilman returned his look. To his surprise, Graf saw no fear in his face, or guilt. The man was inhuman, he thought. They all were. Not a crack in the implacable wall of judgment. It was as if they knew what he was hinting at, and didn't care.

He leaned back in his chair and glared at them. "You can't dictate morality to me, when you've done much worse. You think my little sins of the flesh merit expulsion from the Church, while you have committed much graver sins. The Pope tolerates you because he thinks you are obedient. But if he learns otherwise..." He let them contemplate the unfinished threat and waited.

Graf closely observed the two elderly priests. Nothing was going as planned. Father Herzog and Father Heilman seemed composed. He hated that. He wanted a reaction. He wanted them to be human. Father James's eyes held an intense expression of sadness and compassion.

"The only issue before us is whether you agree to honor the vow of celibacy in order to remain a member of the Society. We need your decision, and we need it before you leave this room."

"Jetzt?! Jetzt gilt es zu entscheiden?" Graf was so angry he reverted to his native German.

"Yes," replied Father Herzog in English. "You must decide right now."

Graf attempted to regain his composure. The muscles of his face convulsed between a grimace and a sneer. He had once respected and admired the men in this room; now he felt only contempt. Why should he have to decide? Why not just lie to them and do what he wanted?

Graf grew suddenly very cold. He felt beaten. If he lied, they would know it. Herzog would pressure him, stare him down. He would get him to the very edge of control, the place where all lies become transparent. Graf felt his anger return. Good. His anger gave him strength.

He swallowed hard and spoke. "My answer is no. But others will agree with me, and will see this as unjust. I've served the Society for years. I do not deserve to be cast out in this manner."

"I'm sorry you feel that way," said Father Herzog in a voice full of sympathy. "Then, as of this moment, you are no longer a member of the Society of Jesus."

Graf stood, turned around and strode toward the door. He turned around again with small jerky movements for a last look at the three priests. His face twisted in a grotesque mask of pain. "You always wanted this. You're happy about this, aren't you?"

"*Nein*," Herzog replied. "*Wir sind nicht froh, sondern traurig, sehr traurig.*"

Father Graf fled the room. He didn't want their damned pity. He grew furious at the thought. They had no right. They thought they had beaten him, but this wasn't over yet. He had all the means he needed to bring them to their knees.

***

"He knows what we did in the war," Father Heilman said quietly after Graf had left. "We defied the Pope's orders. The resistance cell we helped, back in the 1940s. The Jews and Catholics we smuggled out of Germany and Austria. The people…" he faltered briefly. "The people I killed."

"To save the innocent," James reminded him. Father Heilman had confessed the events of the war to him some time ago, and it moved James to know his fellow Jesuit was still troubled by them.

Father Herzog smiled gently. "He believes he can persuade this Pope to turn against us because we defied Pius the Twelfth. We put the Church at risk spiriting people and money out of Germany and Italy, caused innocent priests to be arrested and killed. That is what he'll claim."

"I'm worried about more direct actions he might take," James said. "I know we had to do this now, but…"

Father Herzog laid a hand on his shoulder. "We must know the truth, James. One way or another."

CHAPTER XVIII

Ostia
Wednesday, June 19

"You look like hell, James," Michael said.

"It has been a rough day," James replied.

They stood in the foyer of the villa, Susan next to James, carrying her shoulder bag and a suitcase. Michael tried not to look at her as Helena approached them.

Helena greeted James warmly, with a hug and a kiss on both cheeks. She was radiant in a scarlet sheath, her auburn curls tied back to show off her fine bone structure and amber eyes. She looked exotic, sensuous and vulnerable.

"James," she said. Her Italian accent barely detectable. Only an occasional lilt and the soft roll of her "r's" betrayed her mother tongue. "It's been such a long time. It's a pleasure to see you again." She turned to greet Susan. "And this must be the writer you told me about. Welcome to Ostia, Miss Chambers."

While the two women exchanged pleasantries, Michael gave them a sidelong glance. Susan looked as if the beautiful and self-possessed woman before her was the last thing she'd expected of Michael's wife. Helena was her usual self, playing the gracious hostess. She saw Susan's luggage safely delivered to the house staff, with instructions to put it in the guest room, then suggested they move into the garden.

The summer sun was setting, but lanterns bathed the foliage in golden light. A few well-placed torches kept away insects, a necessity in the summer months. The children were in the garden already, and Michael introduced them. Three year-old Luke made himself understood in the way that all young children did, with gestures and persistence. Six year-old Anthony spoke fluent English, a product of both the excellent English program at St. Bartolome's in Rome and of frequent conversations with his parents. Watching their ease with both guests, Michael felt proud of his boys.

Helena offered Susan a tour of the gardens and the boys ran to a large grassy space with a soccer ball. Luke watched his older brother Anthony with admiration as he kicked. He ran for the ball and returned it to his brother never tiring of the game.

James filled Michael in on Graf's ousting. "It was very hard on me. I once looked up to him. He was strong-minded but fair. But as the years went by, he changed and hardened. He became selfish and materialistic, constantly flouting rules. He became ambitious and impatient."

"But what if Father Graf is your traitor? Wouldn't it be better to keep him close where you can keep tabs on him?"

James gave a slight nod. "I thought about that, too. It's a risk. But it was Father Herzog's decision to make, and we have to send a clear message to the rest of the order, and we need to do it now. Besides, it's been an long time since anyone has been able to keep tabs on Father Graf."

When dinner was ready, they all sat down at a table set up on the terrace. They talked as they ate about Italian politics, the weather, the landmarks of Rome, the beauties of Ostia. Michael barely touched his food, and he strained to act normal. Even when Helena left them for half an hour to put the children to bed, he couldn't relax. His stomach felt as if he had swallowed a large lump of ice.

When Helena returned, James ducked into the kitchen and came out with crystal glasses full of chocolate mousse. He wore a boyish grin as he ceremoniously served the desserts. He radiated wholesomeness and good will. Helena seemed especially delighted by his company. She once told Michael that being around James made her feel protected, the way she'd felt as a little girl playing near her mother.

Susan ate a bite of mousse and gave James a speculative look. "You're celibate. Right?"

Michael stared at her, but James only laughed.

"I'm a priest," he said.

Helena seemed to see her dinner party falling apart and ever the good hostess, she changed the subject. "How many Catholics do you think there are in the world?"

"About seven hundred fifty million, I should think," James answered.

"I had no idea there were so many," Helena said.

"Not so many if you look at the entire world. Buddhists and Hindus outnumber Catholics by at least a billion people."

Susan turned toward James. "But how many Catholics go to church regularly? Not so many in the States these days. Isn't that right, Father?"

His gentle smile didn't waver. "Unfortunately, yes. About fifty-five percent still go to church most Sundays, but twenty years ago it was eighty-five percent. A worrisome trend, I must admit." He glanced at Helena. "And Europe isn't immune. Even here, high divorce rates and family instability are diluting religious attachments."

"It would help if the Church stopped ignoring women," Helena retorted.

Here we go, Michael thought. Helena and James rekindled an old argument: the Church's failure to deal with birth control, female priesthood and the lesser position to which too many clergy relegated women throughout society. He glanced at Susan and saw a slight smile on her face, as if she relished the prospect of verbal combat.

Before he could intervene and turn them toward safer ground, Helena went on. "I find it appalling that the Church claims Mary consented at the age of thirteen to become the mother of God."

"But she did," James said. "There is ample evidence to show she consented."

"Isn't that the classic defense of the pedophile?" Helena asked. "In Christ's time and even today in some countries in the Middle East and India, child marriages are customary. But that doesn't make it right. In Europe and the U.S. we prosecute adults for preying on children. God would be arrested for impregnating a girl below the age of consent."

"People didn't live as long then," James said.

Helena would not back down. "But human biology hasn't changed. My point is she was too young to consent. The brain of a young teenager isn't fully developed."

"The mysteries of the faith require us to have faith," James said.

"Don't hide behind that nonsense. What kind of message is the Church sending to women? Only virgin children are pure? Experienced mothers are impure and unfit to raise Christ? It's creepy and insulting when you think about it, but you would have me suspend rational judgment and just accept something I would tear your eyes out for thinking about my underage sister?"

For a moment, James looked uncertain. Finally he said, "Helena, you sound as if the Church is irrelevant to you."

"No. I do want moral grounding for my children, and I did learn something from my Catholic education. I learned to love and respect my body, and I learned moral and ethical responsibility. But I want my sons to grow up to think for themselves and not to defer to 'mysteries'."

"There is much that is reasonable in Church teachings," James said.

"I don't completely disagree." Helena gave him a mischievous smile. "But don't expect me to take dietary advice from an apple-pushing, talking snake any time soon. The Church is steeped in medieval superstition, but we don't live in those times. Women get educations, we work, and we have the right to vote."

James smiled but gave no ground. "It's good to know some fundamental truth is still being taught," he said. "Perhaps we'll solve the Church's crisis of confidence after all."

Susan interrupted. "Crisis of confidence or crisis of faith? I thought they were the same thing."

James turned toward her. "I mean a crisis of confidence. The Catholic faith is based on love: love of others and of oneself. We are simply spiritual beings having a human experience. Recognizing the spiritual nature of our existence, we realize we are all part of the same universal continuum."

"I agree with that, but it also means viewing women as complete humans of equal value," Helena said.

"But we must not reject the truth along with errors, distortions and degradations that have crept into our dogma over the centuries. The crisis of confidence lies with the clergy, not with the truths in the faith."

Susan savored the last of her mousse. "We've heard from James the priest. What does James the psychiatrist have to say? What is the most fulfilling way to live?"

James leaned forward, elbows on the table. Michael recognized his lecturer's posture: focused and engaged, yet relaxed. James loved to talk about issues like this. Michael began to breathe a little easier. They might get comfortably through the end of dinner after all.

"We must balance our spiritual existence and the constraints of the physical world," James said. "Strive to engage in activities that require constant self-development. Nurture and develop the physical body, but also our spiritual nature. We exist for a purpose: to honor our spirituality. When we do, we cannot help but love others. Hurting others is easily recognized as a crime against ourselves. It's no coincidence that all religions teach this at their core."

His sincerity touched Michael, even as it unsettled him. James spoke so clearly of his life's meaning, turning himself inside out in front of them all as naturally as breathing. Michael knew plenty of men who easily talked about their sex lives, or their incomes and net worth. Some men even talked easily about romantic love. But the love James spoke of was different, love of humanity, love of the spirituality of others. No one else Michael knew, not even other priests, talked about this kind of love except inside a church, and very rarely even then. Spiritual love was the last intensely personal topic; it was the last taboo.

"You still sound like James the priest," Susan said, clearly trying to bait James.

"There is a common assumption that one must conform to labels," James replied mildly, "but I am surprised to hear it from you."

Susan's cheeks, already reddened by wine, turned crimson.

"Psychiatrists and psychologists have recently begun to accept the inseparable links between mental and physical health," James continued. "And one day they will eagerly accept the importance of spiritual health."

"A lot of people don't think like you," Susan protested. "People who think the way you do are asking to become victims. Like Christians thrown to the lions. Anyway, I think priests are hypocrites. They molest children, yet they want to preach to me."

"I don't walk around with blinders," James said. "Honoring one's spirituality doesn't mean letting yourself be victimized by the ugly actions of others. Being savvy enough to recognize and disarm evil does no harm. Thoughts of hate and vengeance do; they harm the spirit and mind and body."

Michael stared at Susan, seeing her clearly for the first time. Here, in his home, she seemed out of place. A child, and not a very polite child at that. Everything he had, his home, his children, his experiences, he'd created with Helena. He'd felt drawn to Susan because she reminded him of Irena and of a past he couldn't change. But she paled like Irena's ghost in comparison to Helena. He realized how much he loved Helena, and how careless he had been.

He glanced at his wife. Helena was watching him intently. Her eyes reflected a stunned blankness, then shock and finally painful awareness.

Michael's stomach felt even worse, as if the lump of ice were melting while his stomach filled with molten lava. He got up, turning away from Helena's gaze, and fought to steady his hands as he poured them all a Frangelico nightcap.

***

Michael opened the bedroom door. Helena stood with her arms outstretched, palms on the wall in front of her, staring at the floor. Her dark hair hung down, hiding her face.

At the sound of his entrance, she lifted her head. Their eyes locked, and Michael felt naked. He went to his wife and took her in his arms, but she pushed him away. "What is going on between you and that woman?"

"Nothing," Michael said defensively.

A flash of pain crossed Helena's face. She wavered, clearly torn between accepting his answer and the instinct that warned her he hadn't told her everything. At first her face held confusion and hurt and her body trembled with her internal struggle. Then she stood still for a moment and imperceptibly shook her head. She stood more erect yet relaxed. On her face was the same expression had seen in Father de Aragon. A willingness to face any truth, however unpleasant, and accept the consequences.

Michael understood for the first time what the expression "terrible beauty" meant. Helen's face was beautiful but terrible because of the relentless honesty that was directed at him under circumstances he'd created. His chest tightened as she locked him in a calm and steady gaze.

"How dare you do this to us?" she said softly. "How dare you make a joke out of our marriage, and a fool out of me?"

Michael flushed. "Nothing happened. There is nothing between me and Miss Chambers. You're imagining things."

"Don't ever tell me I'm imagining things."

"I'm sorry, Helena," he said in a deep soothing voice. "I was attracted to her, but that's all. I swear it. I've just been so confused lately."

Helena turned away and seemed to consider something. Then she turned back toward him, her posture upright and strong.

"Confused," she murmured. Her voice held more power than a shout. "You bet you're confused. But I'll unconfuse you right now. If you want to stay in this marriage, you have to choose. No half way, no back and forth, no maybes, no denials, no lies."

"Helena..."

"Stop," she said firmly. "Susan Chambers can stay here, right here under my nose, right where you put her. But one move in her direction and you're finished. I'll divorce you so fast, I won't have time to take the ring off."

"Helena, if you just let me explain..." *Explain what*, he thought. He couldn't deny he'd considered being unfaithful. She wouldn't buy that. Nothing he said right now would ring true.

He tried again. "You're throwing away ten years of marriage."

"No, Michael. I'm refusing to sully ten years of marriage. You may want to play around with your life, but you can't do it with mine." She jerked her head toward the door. "There's a couch in your study downstairs. Go get yourself a pillow and a blanket." She walked away then, into the adjoining bathroom, and shut the door behind her.

Slowly, Michael left the bedroom. A storage closet down the hall yielded a blanket and pillow. He pulled them out, moving sluggishly as if in shock. In their ten years of marriage, Helena had never made him sleep on the couch. Then again, he'd never given her a reason.

She was right, he realized as he carried his bedding downstairs. It would have been easy to cheat and even easier to walk out if Helena was the kind of woman who blinded herself with half-truths. But she wasn't. In her own way, she was as clear about her life as James was with his. As Michael resigned himself to a miserable night, he realized he had never loved her more, and he had never been more turned on by her.

CHAPTER XIX

Vatican City
Thursday, June 20

Michael drove to the Vatican in his blue Mercedes with James by his side. Michael was getting a tour of the Society's financial trading room, followed by the meeting with the Latin Americans in the late morning. He and James had breakfasted and then ridden in silence for ten minutes. Finally, Michael couldn't stand it anymore.

"James," he said. "What are you trying to do to me?"

"What do you mean?"

"What was the idea, inviting Susan to the villa?"

"Is there any reason why I shouldn't have?"

His innocent tone made Michael angry. "You knew damn well what you were doing. How dare you interfere?"

"Interfere with what?"

Michael was exasperated. This wasn't the way men played the game. He didn't want to be explicit; these things were always tacit. Yet here James was, forcing Michael to spell it out.

Michael's anger evaporated in a sudden rush of shame.

"Your life is coming into focus," James said kindly. "Is that so hard to handle?"

It was hard, he thought. Very hard. James was forcing him to look at his life, to decide what was important to him, to determine his life's meaning. "No one asked you to be my guardian angel," Michael said. "You Jesuits have enough to do, playing the avenging Archangels against the rebellious ones."

James smiled. "Comes with the service. But I'm on your side. I'm a little disappointed that you haven't seen through the other side's attempts at manipulation. It's been right in front of you."

"You said that before. Explain."

"First stop the car and let me drive," James said.

Michael pulled over and changed seats with his friend. James pulled back onto the road and drove slowly through the streets of Rome's outer suburbs. Then he slowed down even more, almost to a stop.

"Look to the right," he said. "What do you see?"

Michael looked out at the streetscape. On a nearby light pole, a placard at eye level held a picture of Susan's face superimposed on a blow-up image of Irena. Michael's jaw dropped. "What is that?" he asked.

"Auto-suggestion," James said. "It's a classic magician's trick to manipulate people into thinking a certain way."

James drove on. About half a mile down the road was a banner wrapped around a pole, printed with the same composite picture of Susan and Irena. Michael saw words under it. "Susan is Irena," he read out loud. A feeling of unreality swept over him as more such images appeared, spaced intermittently along the way to Rome. In a shop window, a mannequin with a honey-blonde wig wore a replica of Irena's favorite blue dress. A placard underneath read SUSAN in bold letters.

"James, this is incredible!"

"Yes. These have been up for weeks. Every time you traveled from Rome to Ostia, or to the Vatican, your subconscious was bombarded with these images."

"But who would go to all this trouble?"

"Someone who knows how important you are to us. Someone with access to your personnel file. Someone who wants you upset and distracted. It can only be our traitor in the Society. Only he would have access to the necessary information."

"Why didn't you tell me sooner?"

"I have faith in you," James said, "and there are some things one has to work through for oneself. Your file is old. Shortly after Irena's death this might have worked, but they underestimated how strong you've grown. And they picked the wrong sort of woman."

Michael realized this was true. He was stronger now. He loved Helena, although he realized he hadn't appreciated her enough.

"It did distract me," he admitted. "Susan already looked like Irena; auto-suggestion just reinforced that. But Susan never met Irena, didn't know how to act like her. And my life has taken a new direction since then anyway."

"Even so, you worried me for a time. These techniques are surprisingly effective."

Michael suddenly felt angry again. The Archangeli used a PSYOP to sucker-punched his psyche. He would have felt less violated if they'd stolen his identity. They had manipulated his thoughts, and that outraged him. He felt manipulated from all sides, though he had to admit that the Jesuits' motives and techniques were more to his liking. Regardless, he wanted his mind back.

A new thought struck him, and he felt a jolt of fear. Susan Chambers was at the villa, with easy access to his family. Was she involved with the Archangeli somehow, or just a dupe? He had no way to know. He took a deep breath and fought for calm. Helena and the boys weren't defenseless, he reminded himself. The Specialists on guard at the villa were easily a match for a lone woman, assuming Susan posed any threat. Helena could hold her own as well. She'd fight like a tigress to protect Anthony and Luke.

***

James led Michael through the computer room, down a narrow hallway and through another large wooden door. They entered a large chamber with about fifty priests and lay people in it, talking into phones and staring at screens.

"Welcome to our securities trading room," James said.

The Society traded actively, James had told him on the way over. They owned a satellite receiver and got *Reuters* for the U.S. market prices and news, *Topic* for the U.K. markets, *Telekurs* for Switzerland and the European market, and *Bloomberg* for additional U.S. market data. Private broker screens linked them directly to trading rooms at the Swiss banks. Their state of the art trading systems were wildly profitable.

Michael walked up to an empty seat. A small nameplate identified it as Father Matteo Pintozzi's old spot. He idly sifted through some papers, then picked up a file that lay near them and opened it. It contained incomprehensible symbols; not computer information, something different. Perhaps a code of some kind. He was so intent on puzzling out the symbols that he started in surprise when he glanced up to see Father Pleurre hovering over him.

"You might have made a little noise," Michael said. He closed the file, but kept hold of it. "Pretty impressive. I've never seen a better designed system."

"And you never will." Father Pleurre gave a satisfied smile. Then his gaze dropped to the file in Michael's hands. His smile vanished. "Where did you get this?" he demanded. "It wasn't here this morning." The agitated priest snatched the file from Michael's hand and leafed through it.

His reaction put Michael on alert. "Right here on Father Pintozzi's desk," Michael replied, keeping his voice calm.

"Did you change the order of the papers in this file?" Father Pleurre barked.

"No." Michael watched the other man closely. "I apologize if there's a problem. James told me I could look through anything I wished."

His courteous reply and unruffled demeanor seemed to mollify Father Pleurre. "I should apologize to you," the priest said, calmer now. "I want you to feel free. I was just surprised to see this particular file here."

"Perhaps the file belonged to Father Pintozzi," Michael said. "He may have been working on something before he died."

Father Pleurre shook his head. "No. The file did not belong to him."

"Whose is it?"

"Mine. Encoded computer passwords. I didn't even know it was missing. I have most of the passwords memorized. I rarely refer to it."

"But Father Pintozzi wasn't in your code group."

"No." Father Pleurre looked even more upset.

Something dropped into place in Michael's head. Before he could nail it down, James interrupted them, signaling them to follow him into another meeting room. They entered the cavernous Papal corridor and walked to a conference room three doors down. Video and slide projectors were set up on one side of the room, and a sheaf of papers marked "Confidential" had been placed at each seat of the unoccupied conference table.

A group of expensively dressed businessmen stood near the table, talking with animated gestures. As Michael entered with James and Father Pleurre, several of the men turned to acknowledge their arrival. Father de Aragon was there as well, along with another middle-aged priest. The two strode toward Michael, the second priest extending his hand.

"Allow me to introduce Father Zavala," Father de Aragon said. "He just returned from South America earlier this morning."

"A pleasure." Father Zavala firmly shook Michael's hand.

Father de Aragon introduced Michael to the Latin Americans. Their names were a roll call of the powerful. Roberto Romito of the wealthy Argentine family; Juan Huerta, whose family owned the Rio Rosa, Argentina's largest bank; Francisco Valle of Argentina; Aldo Dramis of Chile; another Chilean, Juan Lutz, whose family controlled Banco Lutz; Adrian Ibarra, who controlled Grupo Ibarra, the third largest financial group in Mexico; Adrian's cousin Esteban Ibarra, who controlled the Ibarra stock brokerage firm; and Carlos Valentin of the family that owned Banco Valentin in Venezuela. The remaining two men were representatives, one for Eliodoro Campos of Chile's Banco Campos. Emilio Loya, the Mexican industrialist, also sent a representative.

Each of these men represented a cache of personal wealth greater than $1 billion. They controlled key industries and had strong political influence all over Latin America.

The men chatted cordially with Michael for a few minutes, asking polite questions about his background. Each gave Michael a business card and urged him to stay in touch. James took him aside briefly and spoke in a low whisper: "In Latin America, these men are our political and financial cover. They want to get rid of the corrupt priests, tax evaders and other organized crime as much as we do."

After a few more minutes of pleasantries, the meeting began. They were all here, Michael knew, to sort out what the Archangeli had done with the money they took from tax evaders.

Michael scanned through the hardcopy and was ready before the others had gotten through the first few pages. He knew what was in them; he'd compiled the data in the first place. "It seems that the Archangeli were pretty unimaginative in their methods," he said. "They used priests as couriers to carry currency out of the country. A few bought jewelry and smuggled it out. Other tax dodgers made a donation to the Church in their home country, which later showed up as a bank balance for them in another country. The money was transferred directly from a Church account to the accounts of several shell companies, some incorporated in the Vatican, to disguise their true ownership."

"This is an outrage!" The speaker was Carlos Valentin. "The Archangeli funneled some of their funds through Banco Provincial, my family's bank in Venezuela."

"The Church is outraged, as well," Father Pleurre said dryly.

Juan Lutz frowned at the papers in front of him. "This looks extremely complicated. It will take forever to unravel."

"Look in the back," Michael said. "I drew charts showing the flow of money, the companies and their true ownerships." He'd enjoyed that, using his skills as a Ph.D. in finance to untangle the fraud. He often did it for the Specialists. It was fun for him, similar to solving a crossword puzzle.

"They used the Vatican and Liechtenstein to set up most of their phony corporations," Michael went on. "For example,"—he flipped to page five—"this account is set up in the name of RANA Corporation. Apollo Corporation owns sixty percent of RANA, and Delphi Corporation owns forty percent. Tech Corporation owns thirty percent of Apollo, and Mark Corporation owns seventy percent of Apollo. Lana Corporation owns fifty percent of Delphi, as does Capa Corporation."

"You figured that out just by looking at this information?" Lutz asked.

"Here, let me show you." Michael walked over to him and pointed out a chart halfway down the page. "We'll track Tech Corporation's ownership percentage of Apollo, and how that comes from RANA. You'll see here that Tech belongs to Mr. Garsch, a well-known German financier. RANA corporation's only asset is a $1.2 billion cash account in a Basel bank. Of that $1.2 billion, Mr. Garsch's share is thirty percent of Apollo's sixty percent, or $216 million. And that's just in the RANA account. Tech also had part ownership in a few other corporations."

Lutz grunted. "Not so hard after all."

"Consider this," Michael said. "Without the Jesuit information, it would be impossible to unravel this web. These are private corporations. They don't have to disclose anything."

Looking somber, Juan Lutz nodded.

"We have the names of the Archangeli who set up these Swiss accounts," Michael added. "We can link them all the way back to specific tax evaders and deposits. We have the entire ball of wax right here." *Except for Father Miro*, he thought. It troubled him that they still didn't know who the Archangels' leader really was.

One of the Argentines, Juan Huerta, spoke up. "I recognize several Italian Mafia names. Their cash holdings are smaller than those of the Latin Americans, and their money is not mixed in with the others."

"That's right," Michael said. Huerta's speed in catching on impressed him. "Those are probably protection fees, a hangover from their former associations. No one surrounded by Italy can run a racket passing money through Italian banks without a kickback."

As the meeting continued, Michael's satisfaction grew. The Latin Americans were prepared to freeze any listed accounts set up in financial institutions they controlled. They wanted to purge the Vatican of involvement with tax evaders while stinging the tax dodgers. Helping the Jesuits would be a delight for them. They further agreed to freeze the accounts of politicos in Latin in America if they gave the Jesuits a hard time.

At the end of the meeting, a young Jesuit entered with fluted crystal glasses on a tray. Another brought in bottles of chilled Champagne and poured each of them a glass.

"To new friends," Father Pleurre said. "And to a brighter future for our Church."

They raised their glasses and drank.

***

Michael left the Vatican apartments with Father de Aragon and James, eager to get back to his department to monitor the Specialists' preparations for their part in upcoming events. The three men had just stepped into the square filled with tourists when a shot rang out. A bullet struck the pillar just behind Michael's head and ricocheted off the stone into a woman's handbag. She screamed, but was unhurt. Suddenly, everyone within twenty feet of Michael was screaming.

"Get down! Take cover!" Michael shouted. He crouched just as another shot rang out. It whizzed past his left ear.

Father de Aragon dropped down beside him and grabbed both of his arms, placing his own body between Michael and the line of fire. The priest locked eyes with him. "Michael—"

Another shot. Father de Aragon's head exploded like a ripe watermelon hit with a sledgehammer. Bits of shattered bone, pieces of brain and clumps of dark hair splattered across Michael's body. He heard running footsteps all around him as people fled in a stumbling panic for the protection of the colonnade.

James moved to his side, shielding Michael as they moved in swift crab-like fashion behind the nearest pillar. The shots had come sniper-style from up above, across the piazza. Unless there was another gunman, they were safe behind the column of stone.

Michael tried to wrest free of his friend's grasp. He felt sick, his jacket and neck damp with de Aragon's blood and brain matter. "There are more people in the square."

"No." James held him tightly. "There won't be any more shots. The sniper was after you. Without you, the Society can't make its evidence public. The Archangeli's allies in the Italian government and the Mafia are too entrenched for us."

Was James right? Michael wondered if the sniper was after Father de Aragon. Shock and adrenaline kept him from feeling anything yet, but he knew grief for the dead priest would come.

Swarms of Vatican guards flooded the square, several running along the parapet where the shots had originated. They were fast and efficient, but Michael knew they would not be fast enough to catch the sniper.

He and James looked toward the square as the Vatican guards encircled Father de Aragon's body. Everything had happened so fast, it didn't seem real to Michael yet. He felt as if he had watched the entire shooting from a distance.

Father de Aragon was dead. Now Michael knew who Father Miro, leader of the Archangeli, had to be. But he didn't have a shred of proof. He looked down at his gore-spattered jacket and saw a tiny patch of violet. He touched it. It felt soft, silky and warm.

He looked out again at the corpse of Father de Aragon, who had protected him at the cost of his own life. He saw a deformed hand, twisted awkwardly next to the body. He remembered what de Aragon had said about those hands: "The thumb and first two fingers are especially important to me. I can still hold the host to properly say the mass."

Again Michael touched the small patch of violet. Grief struck then, sudden and overwhelming as he realized it was de Aragon's eye.

***

"We must deal with Michael Visconte," Father Miro said. "Our bad luck that he's involved. His family is old money, and he married into another. We don't have our usual leverage."

The Franciscan gave him a sidelong glance. "We have a picture of his wife. We can pick her and the boys up."

"His wife is a Barone. Another powerful family." Father Miro said. "I've kept my name out of things so far, luckily. Still, the Jesuits can prove too much. We have to stop Visconte now."

Selfish bastard, the Franciscan thought. Miro looked out for himself, and to hell with everyone else. "Pintozzi was always a liability," the Franciscan muttered. "For sale to the highest bidder. He sold us information in exchange for a fat position in the Archangeli. He probably turned right around and sold us out for a higher position in the Society." He paused. "If we move quickly, our contacts can put so much pressure on the Viscontes and the Jesuits that they'll back off."

Father Miro nodded. "Once we have his wife and children, Visconte will see the wisdom of leaving things be." He eyed the Franciscan. "Take care of the details."

As always, the Franciscan thought.

CHAPTER XX

Ostia
Thursday, June 20

Helena decided it wouldn't be much of a risk if she drove into Ostia and picked up some fresh fish. Hadn't Michael said the danger was almost over? She liked to choose the fish herself, and she'd just dash in and out. The nanny was watching the children, and she wouldn't be gone more than half an hour. Lorenzo was checking the grounds somewhere, and she hadn't been able to find him after a five-minute search.

She opened the garden gate. Beyond it in the parking area were her BMW, an unmarked car used by the Specialists guarding the house, and a service vehicle for the staff. She was about to close the gate when she heard running footsteps behind her. She turned and saw Susan, hand in hand with Anthony.

"I hope you don't mind," Susan said as they reached her. "Anthony saw you at the gate and said he'd like to go with you. I wouldn't mind a little drive myself. May we come along?"

Helena smiled. "Come along and let your hair down for a while. You always seem to be so busy working."

She'd done her best to be polite to Susan, and was surprised to find she actually enjoyed talking with her the way she enjoyed talking with her young nieces. It was strange to see the woman her husband was attracted to up close. She was curious, and she felt less threatened with the competition safely in her backyard.

Helena put Anthony in the front seat and made sure he fastened his seat belt before she fastened her own and started the car. The tires crunched on the gravel path as they turned toward the access road into Ostia proper.

They reached the first three-way intersection a few minutes later and drove past a dark green Mercedes. It pulled out of the cross-street and fell in behind the BMW.

"I like this countryside," Susan said from the back seat. She rolled down the window and took a whiff of the air. "Mmmm, I can smell fresh-cut grass."

"Haven't you ever smelled grass before?" Anthony asked, with the cheekiness of smart six year-olds the world over. He looked out of the rear window. "That car's following us!"

Helena glanced in her rearview mirror and briefly watched the dark green Mercedes. The car dropped back and its right turn signal flashed. It turned off at the next road.

"False alarm," Anthony said.

"Young boys," Helena said, by way of apology. "They have overly active fantasies."

Anthony corrected her. "Imaginations, mamà."

"Yes, imaginations." Helena said it good-naturedly, knowing Anthony wouldn't give her peace until she repeated it. "If you like the countryside, Susan, wait until you see the beach. I'm going to the fish market there. The water is beautiful, a deep blue-green like a jewel."

"I'm looking forward to it," Susan said.

They arrived at their destination five minutes later. Helena parked the car at a fresh fish stand on the edge of a pristine beach, its beige sand still crowded with late-afternoon sunbathers.

They got out and Helena said she would take Anthony in with her to the fish market. "I don't want you wandering off to play," she told him. "It would take forever to find you in this crowd."

Susan smiled. "I'm not much for fish. I'll just stay near the car and enjoy the view."

***

Susan strolled down the beach for a hundred yards or so, listening to the chorus of Italian voices and observing the etiquette of the beach. Most of the sun worshippers set down blankets and beach chairs under huge vinyl umbrellas. Some were reading magazines or books, eating fruit and exchanging gossip. The beach appeared to be a major social gathering place in Ostia.

Bathing suits were skimpy, she noted; they looked maybe a third the size of those worn on U.S. beaches, and caught the eye with their bold colors and splashy designs. Coconut vendors walked among the noisy crowd plying their wares, and Susan heard the call of "*Fresca Coco*" up and down the beach. The vendors occasionally stopped to accept a euro note and fish a small piece of cut coconut from a bucket of fresh cold water.

Susan watched the beachgoers for a while, and then wondered if Helena might need help carrying her purchases while keeping an eye on Anthony. She turned toward the fish market and froze in horror. Two men in dark clothing were bundling Helena and Anthony into the dark green Mercedes.

Susan ran back to the parking area, but the Mercedes was pulling away as she reached Helena's BMW. As the car sped off, she glimpsed a man in the back seat holding a smartphone to his lips. In his other hand he held a gun on Helena and Anthony.

Susan jumped into the BMW. The keys were still in the ignition. She belted up and screeched out of the parking lot in pursuit.

***

The man with the gun looked past Helena, out the back window of the Mercedes, and swore. He kept his aim rock steady as he fished a smartphone from his pocket.

"Please don't hurt my son," Helena said, never taking her eyes off the gun while their kidnapper punched numbers with his free hand. "If you let him go, I'll do anything you want."

The gunman leered at her. "You'll do anything we want anyway. Just shut up and you won't get hurt. If you annoy me, I'll take it out on the boy."

Helena went quiet, but continued to watch him warily. Anthony looked from his mother to the gunman and back again with wide eyes, but stayed silent.

The man put the phone to his ear. "We have the wife and one boy," he barked. "Another woman was with them. We couldn't find her when we picked up the wife and the boy, so we took off without her. Now she's following us in a BMW. What do you want me to do?"

He paused, as if listening for answer. "All right," he said, and ended the call.

His smug expression deepened Helena's fear. "What are you planning?" she whispered.

He said nothing, merely tightened his grip on the gun.

***

Susan kept one hand on the wheel and groped across the passenger seat. She didn't dare take her eyes from the road, but after a few sweeping motions, she felt what she was seeking: Helena's forgotten cell phone. She opened it and glanced down, then tried the speed dial numbers.

The first number reached the villa. The nanny picked up and Susan asked for one of the Specialists guarding the house. "I'll try to find one," the nanny said, sounding doubtful. *No good*, Susan thought, and tried not to panic.

She hung up and tried the second number, which got her to Michael's office desk in Rome. The man on the other end spoke halting English, and Susan hung up again with her panic mounting.

She tried the third number, and a man answered in Italian. A familiar voice.

"Michael?" she asked.

"Yes," he responded in English. He sounded wary.

"I'm on Helena's mobile phone," she said. "We're in trouble. We went to the fish market in Ostia, and Helena and Anthony were kidnapped. I'm in Helena's car, following them. A dark green Mercedes, license plate EN145. There are two men in it. One of them has a gun."

There was a pause. Then Michael spoke. "All right, Susan." He sounded professional and reassuring. "I'm very near the villa, so you can't be far away from me. I can get to you in no time. Describe the scenery where you are."

She did the best she could. "There's a fruit stand with some writing on it. I couldn't read what it said; I'm going too fast. There's a gas station coming up on my left..."

"Susan," Michael broke in. "Listen carefully. Let me know if you turn off. Don't follow the Mercedes too closely. Keep them in sight, but don't take any risks. They may have accomplices who could make trouble for you. I'm going to hang up now and call my office for help. Don't worry. I'll call you back in a minute and stay on the line with you."

"All right," she said. Ahead of her, the Mercedes sped down the road. No turning off yet.

The phone went dead in her ear. She tightened her grip on it and the steering wheel, and kept driving.

***

Michael hung up, heart hammering against his ribs. Anthony and Helena. What had his wife been thinking, to go out like that with no protection?

He turned to James, who sat next to him in the passenger seat of Michael's car. "I'm going to drop you off on the side of the road," he said. "I'll come back for you later."

James shook his head. "Not on your life. If you're going after them, I'm going with you."

"This is police business," Michael said. "You can't get involved."

"I already am," James said vehemently. "There's no time to lose. Let's go!"

There wasn't time to argue, either. Michael called his office and left short, sharp instructions, then hung up and drove faster.

He wound around the back roads and came out on the main road again, then turned left at a three-way intersection headed into a more sparsely populated area. The BMW and the green Mercedes were nowhere in sight. He dialed Helena's mobile. "Where are you now?" he demanded when Susan answered.

She described the countryside and said the green Mercedes was turning right onto a dirt road.

He knew where she was, he thought. "I'm only a minute or so behind you now," he said. "You're headed to a small stone farmhouse. It's been empty for the last couple of years. They must have set up their headquarters there."

"I see it," Susan said. "There's another dark green Mercedes next to the house. I can't tell if anyone's in it."

***

Michael came around the corner and sped past the BMW. Susan was dimly visible inside. He stopped his car about ten yards from the house and threw himself out, Smith and Wesson in hand, using his open driver's-side door as a shield. He didn't intend to get into a gunfight, but he had no idea what he was up against.

"Hide the gun," James said from behind him. "If they see it, Helena is a dead woman. Our only chance is to look harmless."

Michael eyed the scene in front of him with a sinking heart. James was right. Through the back window of the green Mercedes, he saw a man with a gun pointed at Helena's head.

Michael holstered his weapon and stood. He and James walked toward the farmhouse. The gunman forced Helena and Anthony out of the back seat ahead of him, and Michael saw he carried a snub-nosed .38. As the gunman spotted Michael and James, confusion washed across his face. Clearly, an unarmed male stranger and a priest were the last thing he'd expected.

The driver got out and stood by the car. Michael tensed, then relaxed slightly when he didn't see a gun.

He stepped closer to the gunman, James a few paces behind him.

The farmhouse door opened. Two more men came out, both carrying handguns. They strode toward the cars.

Helena saw Michael then, and her eyes widened. He gave her and Anthony a look of reassurance, but he knew it was a fraud. Four men now, three of them armed, against Michael with his holstered Smith and Wesson. They didn't have a chance.

James stepped between Michael and the two men from the house. The thought of Father de Aragon flashed through Michael's mind; he wanted to scream at James to step aside, but didn't dare make a sound or a move. The men looked surprised to see a priest in their driveway and two extra cars in the entry lane.

As they hesitated, the gunman near Helena let out a piercing scream and clutched his right knee. His weapon slipped from his fingers.

Michael swung into action. He darted forward and pulled Helena and Anthony from the gunman's grasp. He was dimly aware of a scuffle nearby and shouts from the farmhouse, but kept his focus on his wife and son. "Run!" he said, pushing Helena toward the BMW. She grabbed Anthony's hand and they dashed away.

The gunman staggered half upright again, weapon back in hand, and squeezed off an awkward shot. The bullet stung as it grazed the side of Michael's head. Fueled by adrenaline and terror, Michael swept his feet from under him and stomped on the man's face. The gunman's head snapped back with a sickening pop, and Michael heard bones crunch. He wrested the gun from the man's hand and saw the gunman was unconscious, his face a shattered mess.

Michael touched the side of his head. It felt warm and sticky, and his hand came back bright red.

He looked around in time to see James disarm one of the men from the farmhouse. The luckless driver lay sprawled in the dirt at James's feet. James trained the weapon on the second armed thug, who fled toward the parked Mercedes. James fired a couple of rounds at the fleeing man's his legs, but missed. *Lousy shot*, Michael thought. He reached for his Smith and Wesson, then stopped as he realized James was in the line of fire. He lowered his weapon. Michael's own men would eventually pick the bastard up.

The first thug had gotten to his feet, and he threw himself at Michael. The driver staggered up and went for James, who dropped the gun and decked him. It was over in seconds, Michael and James fighting side by side until both their attackers were pinned to the ground. James retrieved the discarded handgun and trained it on the two men. The original gunman, battered by Michael's earlier assault, remained out cold.

Michael stood, wiping mixed blood and sweat from his face. He heard the roar of an engine and looked over toward the cars, in time to see the BMW peel out toward the road. The second green Mercedes, with the remaining thug behind the wheel, sped off after it. Michael swore, drew his gun and fired off a few shots at the retreating Mercedes. He saw at least one bullet hit, but the car didn't slow down.

"Go," James said. His hold on the gun he'd taken never wavered. "I'll keep watch over this bunch."

Michael ran to his own Mercedes and sped off after Helena and her pursuer.

***

Helena saw the green Mercedes bearing down on her. "Hang on," she told Susan and Anthony. "We're going to lose him."

When she reached the turnoff to the main road, she threw the wheel to the right instead of going left. The Mercedes drew up alongside and bumped the BMW. Helena swerved, then bumped back.

Anthony screamed.

Helena downshifted and took the next right turn. The Mercedes screeched behind her, bumping her car's rear. They were fast approaching a narrow bridge, wide enough for only one car. She sped towards it.

As she started over the bridge, she heard a loud bang. The BMW swerved wildly. *Shot out a tire*, Helena thought, choking down panic. She fought for control, but the steering wheel didn't respond. The BMW crashed through the wooden guardrail and plunged toward the stream below.

They hit the water hard. Helena braced herself against the wheel as the car began sinking. Thank God the water wasn't too cold.

"Kick off your shoes," she screamed, and fumbled at her seat belt. The belt gave, and she willed herself to calm down as she climbed into the back seat. Crouching in front of Anthony, she quickly undid his seat belt, then groped under the water for his feet. His shoes were still on, so she pulled them off. Tiny red sneakers.

Anthony was pale, his round eyes brimming. "Mommy, I'm scared," he said in a small voice. He hadn't called her Mommy since he was three years old.

She answered with a calm she didn't feel. "That's all right. I'm here."

Susan, thank heavens, had managed to free herself. "Can you swim?" Helena asked.

"Yes." Susan sounded uncertain. The water had reached her waist, and she looked frightened.

"Don't worry," Helena said firmly. "We're getting out of here. Shoes off?"

Susan nodded mutely.

"All right." She looked Anthony in the eyes. "Take a deep breath and hold it while Susan and I roll down the windows. The water will gush in, but just keep holding your breath. It won't be far to the surface."

Anthony bit his lip. "What about jellyfish?"

"There won't be any jellyfish." She choked back a laugh she knew came from fear. "Just relax and let me hold you. I'll swim you to the top, just like the Little Mermaid. You remember the Little Mermaid?"

Anthony nodded.

The water was halfway up his chest. "All right," Helena said to Susan. "I'll count to three, and then we start rolling." She counted down and then pressed the window-control button.

Nothing happened.

Susan was stabbing at the window button on the passenger side. The window didn't budge. Helena's panic shot higher. The water had shorted out the circuits.

She looked wildly around the car. It had landed at a tilt, and the water hadn't yet breached the driver's side rear window. Sudden calm swept over her, as if she'd gone clear through terror and out the other side. "Never mind, then. I'll kick out that window"—she nodded toward it—"and you follow me."

She pulled Anthony against her, shielding him with her body. "Hold your breath." She grabbed the passenger strap with her right hand and the back seat with her left, took in a deep breath of her own, and slammed both feet against the window. The glass popped out. Water rushed in, crowding out the light as the car sank faster.

***

Racing toward the bridge, Michael heard the shot and watched in helpless panic as Helena's car went through the railing into the murky water. The green Mercedes shot across the bridge and took off down the road.

Michael screeched to a stop hard by the bridge and hurled himself out of his car. He half slid, half stumbled down the river bank toward the water, stripped down to his pants and dove in.

The water was murky, but after a second or two he made out two large shapes in motion. *Anthony*, he thought, and suppressed a jolt of panic. He pushed forward through the current. Relief flooded through him as he saw his son, held close by Helena's arm around his waist. Helena was stroking upward with her free arm and kicking hard toward the surface.

He watched her break through, Susan doing likewise just a few feet distant. Michael swam upward and surfaced just a few strokes away. Anthony was coughing, a blessedly welcome sound. Michael swam over and took Anthony from Helena's arms. Together, Michael and Helena swam to shore. Susan was already there, dragging herself up the bank.

They staggered out of the water. The warm June air and the grassy bank beneath his feet had never felt so welcome. "Cough hard," Helena said to Anthony. "It'll get the water out." Anthony coughed obediently and blew a little water out of his nose, but otherwise seemed unhurt.

Susan stumbled over. "Helena saved us. She kicked out the window and got us out of the car. She saved us."

Michael led them toward his car, parked at a crazy angle by the bridge. His jacket and shirt lay in the grass. He picked the jacket up and wrapped it around Helena and Anthony as best he could. "Forgive me," he said softly.

Helena leaned against him. She looked into his eyes, but said nothing. Then her eyes widened. "You're bleeding."

He'd forgotten about the bullet graze. He picked up his shirt and tore it, then folded the torn strip into a compress for his ear. Helena held it in place. She was shivering despite the jacket, as the adrenaline rush wore off.

"Let's get out of here," Michael said. "Before Mr. Green Mercedes comes back with friends."

***

A few hours later, after hot showers, a change of clothes and a light meal, they gathered around the table on the terrace at the villa. Anthony sat on Michael's lap, clearly enjoying the extra attention from a father reluctant to let him out of his arms. Helena sat next to Michael, Susan and James across from them. Lorenzo, at the far end of the table, spoke softly in Italian with Luke.

"The rest of your men got to the farmhouse just after you left," James said. "They took custody of the thugs and searched the house, but found nothing except a couple more handguns. Colt Trooper Mark III .357 Magnums, to be exact."

"And the one I stomped on?" Michael wanted to know just how badly he'd injured the man. He wanted to know if the man would live.

James looked grave. "He'll live. With a broken neck, though. I expect he'll need reconstructive surgery for his face. Even with the best care, he'll likely be disfigured. And paralyzed. He's paying a heavy price."

True enough, but Michael had no regrets. He gave Anthony a gentle squeeze. His wife and son were alive and unhurt. Even though he knew it wasn't over yet, he felt profoundly grateful. His fellow Specialists had picked up the man in the green Mercedes, who'd been booked for conspiracy, attempted murder, and kidnapping. Michael's villa and the surrounding roads were crawling with Italian security forces.

"We'll retrieve your car tomorrow," he said, with a wry glance at Helena. "We'll probably have to get a new one."

She returned his smile. "This time I'll just kick the tires."

James examined Michael's head wound. "When was the last time you had a tetanus shot?"

He had to think about it. "Last year."

"I think you should get antibiotics and an X-ray just to be on the safe side. You might need a stitch or two, although it doesn't look too bad."

"One thing I'd like to know," Michael said, "is what happened to that gunman in the first place. When he screamed and grabbed his knee. Something hurt him, but I didn't see what."

Anthony turned and looked up at Michael. "I did. I kneecapped him!" The boy's face shone with pride.

"What?" Michael was stunned. "How?"

"He was going to hurt mamà. He was a bad man. I had my whittling knife Lorenzo gave me. So I stuck him."

Michael kissed the top of his son's head. "You may have saved all our lives."

***

Helena took the boys off to bed a little later, clearly unwilling to relegate that task to the nanny on this particular night. Michael reluctantly let his older son go. He felt proud of Anthony, but also unsettled. A six year-old boy never should have been in that kind of situation, defending his mother from an armed thug.

James had gone into the house, leaving Michael and Susan alone on the terrace. He saw his opportunity and took it. "You set me up," he said.

She looked startled, then shamefaced. "Yes, I did. "I'm sorry about that now."

"It was Graf," wasn't it?"

Her eyebrows rose. "How did you know?"

"I smelled your perfume in his apartment." It had taken him awhile to place the scent, but he was sure of his ground now. "Why did you do it?"

Susan tossed her head and shrugged. "Graf said he'd give me inside information on what was happening in the Vatican. I'd have a great story about a major change in the Catholic Church, with power struggles, murders, pictures, background material, everything."

"And that was all?" Michael asked gently.

Susan looked away. "He also paid me $25,000. He bought me clothes and paid for my dye job. He said it was important that I look right." She fidgeted with her hair. "I'm sorry. I had no idea there would be any real danger."

Money and a story, he thought. Graf had gone to great lengths to throw him off balance. He had access to Michael's files, to pictures of Irena. The sense of violation made Michael furious. And Susan was a willing accomplice. He couldn't bring himself to forgive her, at least not yet.

"Well, what exactly did you think was going to happen?" Michael couldn't hide his irritation. "You agreed to be an accomplice in an obvious scam."

Helena stepped out on the terrace and heard his last remark. Her expression was grave and tense. She approached them with a keen glance at Susan before turning to Michael. "You have a phone call," she said. "A Father Graf. He says it's urgent."

Michael strode into the house and picked up the phone. "Yes?"

Graf's deep voice came over the line. "I know who Father Miro is, and I have evidence that can help you. Can you meet me at my apartment at nine?"

Michael glanced at his watch. Two hours from now.

He made a swift decision. "I'll be there."

"Come alone," Graf said.

CHAPTER XXI

Rome
Thursday, June 20

Father Graf's door was ajar when Michael arrived at the priest's apartment. He drew his gun, pushed the door open wider, and cautiously stepped inside. It appeared quiet and deserted.

Graf's dining room looked ready for an *Architectural Digest* photo shoot. The elegant china, silver and crystal service were arranged for a formal multi-course meal for two. A candelabra centerpiece held fresh white tapered candles, unlit. A wine bucket held water with remnants of melting cubes.

He called Father Graf's name. "It's Michael Visconte. Are you here?"

No answer. Gun at the ready, Michael moved swiftly and carefully through the apartment.

In the kitchen, a large saucepan held veal scaloppini, the sauce cold and congealing around the meat. The bedroom and bathroom were empty and undisturbed. Not even a faint trace of perfume.

In the study he found a note, hastily written on a piece of stationery: *Change of plans. Meet me at the top of the Castel Sant'Angelo.* Michael stared at the note for a second or two, then quickly went through Graf's desk. The priest's appointment book yielded several handwritten scrawls that matched the writing on the note.

Michael took his phone from his pocket and dialed his office. He relayed some quick instructions, tucked the phone away, and headed for his car.

***

Michael carried no flashlight, but the city below provided just enough light for him to dimly make out his surroundings at the top of the Castel. He saw the burly priest waiting for him, leaning against the base of the dark angel's statue. The priest stayed silent and immobile, as if waiting for Michael to come to him.

The hair stood up on the back of Michael's neck. He knew Graf was Father Miro, the Society's traitor and capable of murder. Graf had ordered the killings of Father Manion and Father Pintozzi, and Michael suspected he'd disfigured Manion's body under the guise of the autopsy. He'd likely ordered Father Pintozzi's mutilation too. But Michael couldn't prove anything unless he trapped Graf into incriminating himself. All he had was a folder full of coded passwords on Pintozzi's old desk. Father Pleurre's passwords, which Pintozzi hadn't known. Which in turn meant the traitor to whom Pintozzi fed information was Father Graf or Father de Aragon, until de Aragon's death left only one suspect.

He tightened his grip on his gun and took a slow, deep breath. It was down to him now, and to whatever happened in the next few minutes. He owed it to his family, to James, to Father de Aragon, to the Specialists and to himself.

He approached Father Graf. The priest didn't move. He gazed unblinkingly at Michael, who felt new fear as the meaning of that eerie stare sank in.

Graf's face was oddly smooth, lacking the grimace of a death mask. Michael moved closer and saw that the priest had been stabbed through the heart. The stain around the wound was surprisingly small. Dead for less than an hour, Michael guessed.

A savage blow came down hard on Michael's bandaged head. The impact drove him to his knees. He rolled away, ears ringing, and tried to right himself. A savage kick to his ribs knocked the wind out of him. Before he could draw breath, another kick sent him sprawling.

Rough hands raised him, pulling him toward the edge of the battlements. Too dazed and winded to fight, he let himself sag. Dead weight would make things harder for his attacker.

"You shouldn't have gotten involved," a familiar voice said. Michael blinked and focused on the face of Father Pleurre. "It's too bad you showed up here."

Shock coursed through him. He had to buy time, clear his head. Stay alive long enough for his men to arrive. "Why?" he managed to gasp.

"Graf betrayed the Society. I tapped his telephone and his computer; I know everything. He called me tonight, begging me to use my influence to help him. But he lied. He was going to frame me as the traitor! I told him to meet me here, where no one could see us who might make more trouble for him. He believed me. It was so easy to trap him." Father Pleurre chuckled, a chilling sound. "I can protect the Society. I have devoted my life to it. Evil men like Graf, like Matteo Pintozzi—I won't allow them to destroy it."

"Pintozzi?" Michael's breath came easier now, though he still felt too dizzy to best Pleurre in a fight. Just a minute longer... "You killed him?"

"He was a traitor as well," Pleurre growled. "A parasite feeding on other men's wounds of the spirit. He charmed me at first, the way he charmed everyone else. He flattered me, said he couldn't have made so much money without me. A few months ago, he asked me to be his confessor. He told me he was a homosexual. A disgusting little pervert. And he took things, confidential papers, secure computer files. He gave them to someone in the Archangeli. I didn't know who then, but I knew I had to act."

"You were wrong," Michael said. He felt his strength returning. "Father Pintozzi wasn't a traitor. He was acting on Father Herzog's instructions."

"Liar!" Pleurre spat the word and shook Michael hard.

"No." Michael fought off a new wave of dizziness. "He was helping to unmask the Archangeli. Father Pintozzi infiltrated the computer system just far enough to earn their trust, so he could discover who their leader was."

Father Pleurre stared at Michael in confusion.

"It's over, Father," Michael said. "My men are all around the Castel by now, on their way up here."

"I don't believe you," Father Pleurre croaked, his face twisted in agony and doubt.

"Father Pintozzi was loyal to the Society. You made a mistake. You harmed the Society and killed an innocent man."

"No, I would never harm the Society!" Pleurre choked out a wail of grief. *Matteo was a traitor!*"

He dragged Michael nearer the edge of the battlements. Head throbbing, Michael struggled in his grip. He was losing ground, moving nearer to the edge.

Pleurre gave a final, powerful shove. Michael allowed his body to go limp, dropped his weight straight down towards the masonry, and used his attacker's own momentum against him as he grabbed the priest and threw him. Father

Pleurre hurled past him and vanished into the darkness below.

CHAPTER XXII

Vatican City
Friday, June 21

Father Herzog meditated and prayed. He performed the Spiritual Exercises and the Jesuit Test of Conscience, and asked for strength and guidance in the task he was about to undertake. Then he dressed in the simple black robes of a Jesuit priest and assessed himself in the mirror. His white mane testified to his advanced years, but his posture was youthful and erect. A leather briefcase held his carefully prepared documents, and he picked it up. He took a last deep, calming breath and left his rooms, making his way swiftly to the Apostolic Palace.

At the entrance to the Papal apartments, he was briefly stopped by the first set of guards, who examined but did not attempt to read the contents of his briefcase. The other three sets of guards waved him on through. He was expected.

At the door to the Papal reception room, the *Maestro di Camera* showed him in, with a curious glance at Father Herzog's briefcase. Herzog smiled, but declined to enlighten the man. He knew there was intense speculation in the

Vatican as to why the Superior General of the Society of Jesus had requested a special private audience with the Pope, let alone on such short notice. Such a thing had never happened before in the memory of the Vatican. The *Maestro di Camera* strained to hear Father Herzog's words. He closed the soundproof door as slowly as decency would allow.

"*Salve clementissime Papa*," Father Herzog said. "*In spiritu humilitatis, et in animo contrito suscipiamo a te, Pater.*"

The *Maestro di Camera* frowned in disappointment. All he heard was a flowery Latin greeting: Hail, gracious Father, may you accept my spirit of humility and contrite heart."

The Pope was waiting for Herzog at a small table. Father Herzog greeted him and took the empty seat. The Pope and Father Herzog continued with the polite Latin formalities.

Herzog took a moment to focus, and imagined what the two of them must look like. The hulking Pope in white ceremonial robes, Herzog himself—thinner and smaller but sturdier—in his simple black cassock. Two white-haired old men with the fate of their Church in their hands.

Father Herzog looked at the Pontiff and switched from Latin to flawless upper-class German. "With the permission of Your Holiness, I would like to continue the rest of this meeting in Your Holiness' mother tongue."

The Pope's eyes widened slightly, a subtle betrayal of surprise. After a moment, he nodded stiffly. "Please continue."

Father Herzog reached for his black briefcase and took out two sets of documents. He handed one to the Pope and kept the other. "If it please Your Holiness, this is a detailed listing of the Archangeli, their conspirators, and proof of their participation in criminal activities."

The Pope's expression betrayed nothing. "Why are you bringing Us this information, Father Herzog?"

"The Society thinks it is important these crimes be brought to Your Holiness' attention. Obviously this has serious ramifications for the administration of the Church."

They sat in silence for several seconds, Father Herzog unruffled by the Pope's cold appraisal. It bothered the Pontiff, Herzog knew, that he himself spoke the perfect German of an orator, rather than the Pope's lower middle-class German. He was counting on that to add to the intimidating effect of the information the Pope held in his hand.

"We think this is a matter for Vatican Intelligence," the Pope said. "We must insist the Society turn over all of its evidence to Us. We stress *all of it*, and We will take care of it from here."

"I am afraid that is no longer possible, *Papa*." Father Herzog used the Latin term for the Pope, making it sound like a childish nickname.

The Pope's face reddened and he glared at Father Herzog. "If you cannot turn over all the evidence, there must be a good reason, and We are prepared to hear that reason now."

Calmly, Father Herzog delivered his bombshell. "We—and by 'we' I don't mean the Papal 'We,' I mean The Society—have already turned over copies of the evidence to the Specialists in Rome. The Specialists are in the process of distributing information to the international press."

The Pope clenched his hands around the documents. "What possessed you to do a thing like that? You should have come to Us first. This is a disaster! Why did you do it?"

Father Herzog gave his best guileless smile. "Because I knew Your Holiness could not rest unless this corruption and those guilty of it were exposed once and for all."

"*We* should have made that decision. *We* rule in the Vatican."

"Without doubt, Your Holiness rules in the Vatican," Father Herzog said evenly. "It is a shame that so many of these crimes occurred off Vatican soil and broke laws in other countries. From that list, Your Holiness can see that many of the perpetrators are now in the United States, Italy, Switzerland and Latin America."

The Pope stared long and hard. Father Herzog waited, calm and sure of himself. After several seconds, the Pope's stiff posture sagged slightly. "What do you suggest We do next?"

Father Herzog reached again for his black leather briefcase. He took out three additional documents and a gold pen, and set them down. He rose and walked to the Pope's private desk, took up the Papal seal, returned to his chair and placed the seal next to the pen on the table in front of him. Then he picked up the documents.

"I suggest Your Holiness write a Papal encyclical giving broad administrative powers, including the power of excommunication, to the Society. We have taken the liberty of drafting one. If Your Holiness approves, Your Holiness need only sign these documents and affix the Papal seal. I have provided Your Holiness with three translations: one in German, one in Latin and one in English. Father Heilman is waiting outside this room to act as another witness."

Father Herzog handed the German version to the Pope. The Pope took it as if it were a small dead animal. He read through the document, and when he looked up, his face showed fear.

"You are asking to preempt the tribunal of Cardinals," the Pope said, his voice shaking. "You are asking for broad powers to police the other Orders. You are asking Us to authorize a Jesuit Rota. And you ask for Our censure of sexual activities by members of the clergy, in effect admitting their wrongdoing."

"I realize it is a lot to digest in one sitting," Father Herzog said. "Take all the time Your Holiness needs, but I urge Your Holiness to sign sooner rather than later."

The Pope's voice hardened. "You have gone mad. Why would We relinquish this much power to the Jesuits?"

"Because Your Holiness cannot pay Your Holiness' bills," Father Herzog said, as he took one last sheet of paper from his briefcase and handed it over. "We have diverted all of the money from Vatican-related accounts to a temporary safe place. We are prepared to give it back as soon as Your Holiness signs these papers."

The Pope scanned the paper. He turned a deeper red and his eyes bulged. "Thieves!"

"The Vatican is no stranger to theft. I recall us paying $250 million in reparations to Banco Ambrosiano after the embezzlement three decades ago."

Father Herzog sat back in his chair. He took up the encyclicals and held them out, his gaze never leaving the Pope's. He watched a succession of impulses play across the Pontiff's face: throw Herzog out, call the guards, defy him and the Society somehow. Then, finally, reality sank in. The Pope looked down at the paper in his hand, then back to the encyclicals Father Herzog held. He hesitated a full minute and then took the documents with trembling hands.

Father Herzog called to the *Maestro di Camera*. The bishop entered the room so quickly, Father Herzog knew he had stayed right by the door. Trying to listen, probably. "Please show Father Heilman in," Father Herzog said smoothly in Latin, as the Pope picked up the gold pen. "We are ready for him now."

CHAPTER XXIII

Ostia
Friday, June 21

Michael struggled to find a comfortable position in the shower. Everything hurt. He had gratefully gone to the emergency room after his encounter with Father Pleurre. He'd luckily avoided serious injuries, but his ear and scalp needed stitches, and two painful broken ribs sported tape. His head and face were bruised and swollen in spots, and deep breaths caused him stabbing pain.

He lathered his arms, trying to keep the adhesive on his ribs dry. A sudden noise almost made him drop the soap.

Through the shower door's wavy glass, Michael saw Helena enter the bathroom. She wore only a towel. She came over, and her towel slipped to the floor as she opened the shower door and stepped in beside him.

The sight of her made him forget his pain. "Good morning," Michael said with a huge grin.

"Good morning, yourself." Helena reached for the soap. She lathered herself quickly, then rubbed against him.

He loved the feeling of the warm water cascading down his back and her slippery body next to his. She smelled clean and fresh. They stood pressed against each other with the water raining down on them. Michael knew his tape was getting wet, but he didn't care anymore.

Helena pressed her hips against him. He kissed her long and hard on the mouth, and felt himself grow hard against the lower part of her stomach. His hands slid down her back, then up around her breasts and back down between her legs. Before she could move his hand away, he began rubbing her in deft circular motions. He laughed with pleasure at her moans when she reached a shuddering orgasm. She tried to reciprocate, but he wouldn't let her. They rinsed off the soap and quickly toweled each other off, and Michael led her into the bedroom.

They made love, moving carefully because of his ribs, both of them taking their time. "Michael," Helena said after they'd gathered their strength.

"Yes?"

"I drove Susan to the airport."

He nodded, suddenly almost afraid to speak.

They both said nothing for a few moments. Finally Helena spoke again. "Michael, did you think all of this was an accident?"

He didn't understand. "All of what?"

"Happiness. The way we live our lives, the way our children are, the way our home is, the way our employees respect us, the good friends we have, our marriage. None of that is an accident. It comes from the conscious decisions we make every day of our lives."

He hadn't thought about it quite like that before, but he realized he had been happy. Between his career and his other responsibilities, he'd simply taken it all for granted. "I know," he admitted finally. "For a long time, I've just been along for the ride."

"But no more," Helena said firmly. "If you're in, you're in one hundred percent."

He shifted position, ignoring the sharp twinges in his side, to look directly at her. "One hundred percent."

He expected her to smile, but she didn't. She looked at him as if analyzing a problem, distant and dispassionate. A chill of anxiety ran down his spine.

"After this case is prosecuted, I'm leaving the Specialists," he said. "You were right. The risk isn't worth it."

"Do you think it's as simple as that? A little sex, a few words and all is forgotten? After everything that's happened, I'm not sure I know who you are, Michael. But I'm willing to give you a chance."

"A *chance*. Helena, I'm your husband."

Her expression then made Michael sit up. "Only when it suits you," she said coolly. "You've acted like a guest in this house. You've put all our lives in jeopardy. You've left the makings of this family to me, and I nearly saw it destroyed." She glanced away from him, then turned back and rested her hand on his. "I'll give you a chance, Michael, but I want to see if you can go the distance."

CHAPTER XXIV

Vatican City
Saturday, June 22

Father James looked around the conference table at the remaining members of the Rota. They had won; they could operate with virtual carte blanche under the Pope's authority. The leaders of the other Orders had been contacted and stood ready to support the Jesuits. But the cost was enormous. The Rota now numbered only nine, and they had another decision to make.

Father Herzog spoke. "Early this morning, all of the money in the Archangeli accounts reappeared in the Society's accounts. Shortly afterward, the Archangeli found that all of their data had been destroyed. Nothing was left but a message flashing on their computer screens: '*Ad majoram Dei gloriam*.'"

Father Aiello made a sound halfway between a laugh and a sigh. "One of Saint Ignatius' favorite mottos. All their friends will think the Archangeli double-crossed them. Unless they can trace it back to us?"

James smiled. "Unlikely. They're preoccupied trying to save themselves."

Father Herzog went on. "I have ordered all members of the Archangeli in Latin America back to the safety of Rome, so they cannot be prosecuted or harmed by their tax dodging friends. We will excommunicate them, and then release them in Italy. "Our Latin American friends, meanwhile, will help us clean house and reclaim the Church. So now, only one question remains: What do we do with the money from the Archangeli accounts?"

"We keep it," Father James replied.

All eyes turned toward him. "The way things now stand," he continued, "we can't hurt anyone in the Archangeli by keeping it. I can't see returning money to tax dodgers. If they complain, they may expose themselves. And the Society can use more cash right now."

A murmur ran around the table. "What about taxes?" Father Aiello asked.

Father James gave a broad smile. "Have we ever paid taxes on donations to the Church?"

CHAPTER XXV

Ostia
Sunday, June 22

Father James said a family mass at the villa, and afterwards he and Michael sat in the shade of a trellis on the terrace. The breakfast table was set with bone china and held platters of fresh fruit, croissants, and boiled eggs. James poured himself some freshly squeezed orange juice. "Now that you've solved your case," he said, "what do you intend to do with your life?"

"We still have to prosecute. There's still a lot of work to be done."

"But after that?"

"I'm leaving the Specialists, but beyond that, I haven't had time to give it much thought." Michael said. He watched James peel a blood orange. "Did you know about Father Pleurre?"

"I guessed. I warned the Society, but they didn't believe me, and I had no proof. Only suspicions, and a diagnosis that made him among the most dangerous types of people. A malignant narcissist. But a diagnosis is both art and science. There is room for error, and I was overruled."

Michael knew the term. He had taken a criminal psychology course as part of VICAP, the Violent Criminal Apprehension Program, at the FBI National Academy in the United States. They taught foreign counter-intelligence to law enforcement officers from all over the world.

James went on. "Narcissists have poor self-esteem, but they are typically very successful. They feel entitled; they're self-important; they crave admiration and lack empathy. They are also exploitative and envious. The malignant types never forget a slight. They may kill you ten years later for cutting them off in traffic. But they act perfectly normal while plotting their revenge."

"When Father Pleurre thought Father Matteo had betrayed the Society, it must have felt personal," Michael said.

"I think it was more than that." James took a deep breath. "I think Father Pleurre wanted Father Matteo's admiration. Father Pleurre may well have been a latent homosexual, but he couldn't admit it to himself. So he jumped to the wrong conclusion that Father Matteo betrayed the Society, partly to justify murdering him for a slight he couldn't acknowledge. He wanted Matteo. But Matteo was oblivious to his interest."

"He was enraged when I confronted him," Michael said. "He couldn't accept that Matteo wasn't a traitor."

James finished the orange and helped himself to a croissant and eggs. "At any rate, now the Society needs someone to replace Father Pleurre. Someone more balanced. We were thinking of recruiting outside the clergy for the job. Perhaps a family man." He grinned at Michael. "I believe you'll find it very lucrative."

Michael thought about the implied offer. Managing enormous wealth with the kind of edge the Jesuits could offer was a once-in-a-lifetime opportunity. He could keep his promise to Helena and have the job of his dreams. With the kind of wealth he was being offered and connections unmatched by anyone, he'd have power to rival the U.S. Federal Reserve Bank, the most influential financial institution in the world. "It's tempting," he said finally.

He looked across the garden, where Helena played with Luke and Anthony. He didn't want to give James an answer just yet. He wasn't sure how much of a commitment he wanted to make to the Jesuits or to the Church.

"This has been a difficult time for the Society. We're saying a requiem mass next week to again mourn the deaths of all of our fallen Jesuits. Will you come?" James asked.

"Yes, of course I'll attend." Michael scanned his friends face for any sign of regret, but found none. "I hope it was all worth it. You have everything you wanted: control of the Vatican Bank, control of the congregation's global finances, and the authority of the Pope to clean house."

"No," said James. "This is just the beginning. We have much bigger plans."

Michael took care not to bump his sore ribs against his armrest as he turned to face James. "What do you mean by much bigger plans?"

"Come to the mass and after that we'll meet again with Father Herzog." James refused to say more.

They sat for several minutes watching Luke and Anthony play and listening to the summer sounds of splashing water and the boys' excited voices.

James followed Michael's gaze with a knowing smile. "You seem very far away."

"No, I'm not far away at all," Michael said. "But I have a long way to go. A very long way. I need to see if I can go the distance."

"And where will you end up?"

"I'm not sure," Michael answered. "But I have the feeling the best is yet to come."

Afterword

Although this is a work of fiction, references to the Vatican Bank financial scandal in the 1980's, the 1982 murder of Roberto Calvi, and the present day prosecution of priests in the United States for sex crimes against children are inspired by actual events.

In 1974, the crash of Franklin National Bank was the largest in the history of the United States. The Vatican Bank lost $55 million when Franklin collapsed. Michele Sindona, a Franklin National Bank officer, ran a money-laundering operation for Sicilian and U.S. Mafiosi, and he was sentenced to twenty-five years in the Otisville U.S. Federal prison. A United States Comptroller of the Currency's report unearthed the secret account of "Big Paul" Castellano, underboss of the Gambino crime family. At the time Sindona was internationally famous for his bold financial crimes. His marriage also got a lot of press, as did his several mistresses.

When Sindona's friend Roberto Calvi, the chairman of Banco Ambrosiano—also known as "the priests' bank"—turned his back on him, Sindona told Italian banking authorities to start investigating Calvi's foreign special purpose corporations and links to the Vatican Bank.

Paul Casimir Marcinkus was born in 1922 in Cicero, Illinois, Al Capone's neighborhood. By 1969 he had risen within the Catholic Church to become Archbishop of Orta and Secretary of the Roman Curia. Marcinkus was a hulking, charming American of Lithuanian heritage. His lucky break arrived in November 1970 when a knife-wielding would-be assassin lunged at Pope Paul VI during a papal tour in the Philippines. Marcinkus tackled the assassin, saved Pope Paul VI's life, and instantly became a shooting star in the Vatican. The grateful Pope appointed Marcinkus head of Vatican intelligence and security. In 1971, with Cardinal Spellman's backing, Marcinkus became head of the Instituto per le Opere di Religione, the Institute of Religious Work, better known in Europe as the IOR and in the United States as the Vatican Bank. He remained in that post until 1989. In 1981 he was appointed Pro-President of Vatican City, the third most powerful person in the Vatican, a sixth of a square mile sovereign state surrounded by Italy. Marcinkus attended a wedding for Michele Sindona's daughter in the Caribbean. Marcinkus also knew Roberto Calvi, whose links with the Vatican Bank inspired Calvi's nickname, "God's Banker." The Vatican Bank facilitated some of Calvi's shady business dealings.

After Pope Paul VI died in August 1978, the College of Cardinals elected Albino Luciani, the Cardinal of Venice. He ascended to the papal throne as Pope John Paul I. It was rumored the new Pope was furious with Marcinkus. Marcinkus had sold the profitable Venetian Bank, Banco Cattolica del Veneto, to Roberto Calvi over the then-Cardinal Luciani's vehement objections. Luciani was said to have vowed that if he became Pope, he would put an end to Archbishop Marcinkus's power and influence over Vatican affairs.

Pope John Paul I didn't have a chance to implement his plans; he unexpectedly died on September 28, 1978 after reigning only thirty-three days. Vatican intelligence said he died of natural causes, even though he was reputed to be in good health. Speculation over the cause of his death inspired a scene showing the murder of the Pope in the movie, *The Godfather Part III.*

Pope John Paul II's October 1978 election was a stroke of luck for Marcinkus. The Polish Pope was initially an outsider in the Vatican power structure; he was the first non-Italian Pope since Hadrian VI in 1522. Marcinkus and the Pope became fast friends, and the Pope became one of Marcinkus's supporters. In 1982 Marcinkus foiled an assassination attempt against Pope John Paul II in Fatima, Portugal. By then Marcinkus was implicated in Mafia-linked financial scandals splashed on the front pages of European newspapers.

The Vatican Bank set up dummy subsidiaries for Roberto Calvi's Luxembourg holding company, and Marcinkus was on the board of some of them. These subsidiaries were located in several countries, including Switzerland, Liechtenstein, Panama and the Bahamas. Roberto Calvi was accused of embezzling money from Banco Ambrosiano's depositors. These subsidiaries lent millions of the bank's money to Panamanian special—very special—purpose corporations owned by the Vatican Bank.

Banco Ambrosiano collapsed in 1982, and $1.3 billion was missing. The Vatican Bank paid a $250 million settlement to the defrauded depositors of Banco Ambrosiano, but admitted nothing except a "recognition of moral involvement." Though Archbishop Marcinkus had studied canon law in Rome and was head of the Vatican Bank for ten years, he claimed he never read or understood the documents he signed. He said he trusted Roberto Calvi, whom he blamed for taking advantage of his naïveté.

Roberto Calvi was subsequently imprisoned for illegal foreign money transfers. After being released on appeal, Calvi fled to London carrying a briefcase stuffed with incriminating documents. Flavio Carboni, another bank officer, joined him. Shortly after his arrival in London, Roberto Calvi's corpse was found hanging under Blackfriars Bridge. His pockets were stuffed with rocks, and it was rumored his wrists looked as if they had been bound with rope that was later removed. At the time, it was officially deemed a suicide. Carboni and the documents were missing.

Carboni later resurfaced. Italian officials arrested him attempting to extort $900,000 from Vatican officials in exchange for Calvi's stolen documents. Bishop Pavel Hnilica, a key member of Marcinkus's inner circle, was also arrested as he tried to buy back the incriminating documents.

In 1998, Italian investigators performed a new post mortem examination of Calvi's remains using modern forensic techniques. The examiners concluded that Calvi's murder was staged to look like a suicide. He had been strangled and then strung up on the scaffolding under London's Blackfriars Bridge.

Licio Gelli, a former "grand master" of the illegal P2 Masonic lodge, was indicted and acquitted. Gelli acknowledged Calvi was murdered, but claimed the "execution" was ordered in Poland for Calvi's alleged financing of the Solidarity trade union at the behest of Pope John Paul II. Four others were also indicted in 2005: Flavio Carboni, who had fled with Calvi to London; Manuela Kleinszig, Carboni's Austrian girlfriend; Ernesto Diotavelli, an underworld figure from Rome; and Pippo Calo, a boss of the Cosa Nostra, already in prison for other crimes. Prosecutors suspected Calvi knew too much about the laundering of Mafia money through the Vatican Bank and Banco Ambrosiano, but all suspects were subsequently acquitted.

Even for those innocent of any wrongdoing, the murder of someone they know and with whom they have transacted business imposes a moral obligation to come forward and tell what they know about what might have led to the crime. But this has not been the position of the leaders of the Catholic Church.

Archbishop Paul Marcinkus was indicted by Italian authorities during the investigation of Banco Ambrosiano's collapse, but he was never arrested. He lived in the Vatican for six years during the papacy of John Paul II, never stepping foot in Italy, where he would have been apprehended. Eventually the Vatican came to an agreement with Italy to drop the charges. Marcinkus returned to the United States in 1990 and retired to Sun City, Arizona, where he died of undisclosed causes at the age of 84.

But murder and suspicious financial transactions are not the only crimes on which the Catholic Church has remained silent. Scores of priests and former priests in the United States are accused of pedophilia and of having sexually abused children over a period of decades. Catholics in the United States are outraged, and only 3,300 seminarians are currently studying to become priests. The number has dropped by two-thirds from what it was forty years ago.

In 2003, CBS News obtained a secret Vatican document written in 1962 by Cardinal Alfredo Ottaviani. It called for absolute secrecy about sexual abuse perpetrated by priests, although it referred to sexual assault or attempted assault of children of both sexes and of sex with animals.

The document labeled this cover-up a secret of the Holy Office, and it warned that anyone who revealed these secrets would suffer excommunication. In the summer of 2002, the Church drafted new policies meant to address what had become a crisis in the Church.

On May 8, 2002, Cardinal Bernard Law of Boston became the first Cardinal in the history of the Catholic Church to be forced to testify in a sexual abuse case about his role in overseeing priests. Although forced to resign as Archbishop, he presided over Pope John Paul II's requiem mass in 2005. Many U.S. Catholics viewed his presence at the ceremony in shocked disbelief.

In April 2005, German-born Joseph Alosius Ratzinger became Pope Benedict XVI, the 265th head of the Catholic Church. His teenage membership in the Hitler Youth was controversial even though the young Bavarian was required to join by law. He was later a draftee in the German army and a POW of Allied forces. As a cardinal, Ratzinger was part of investigations into sex scandals and seemed more eager than Pope John Paul II to impose sanctions. In his role as Pope Benedict XVI, he has expressed a firm resolve to clean up the sex abuse and "filth" in the Catholic Church, demonstrated by his forcing Maciel Degollado, a Mexican priest, out of the church. Father Maciel founded the Legion of Christ, and the Pope pressed an investigation into that order and its lay arm, the Regnum Christi. He also pressed other international investigations and imposed guidelines directing the Church to follow the new norms established by U.S. bishops as well as local civil laws.

Yet even the financial scandals continue. In July 2012, *Der Spiegel* reported that the Vatican Bank is allegedly engulfed in another scandal involving suspect money transfers and dodgy bank accounts. Gotti Tedeschi, former head of the Vatican Bank and Pope Benedict XVI's confidant, was detained by Carabinieri, Italy's military police, in a corruption investigation involving an Italian subsidiary of Spain's Banco Santander. Among Tedeschi's files was evidence allegedly suggesting Church complicity in circumventing European money-laundering rules. Details of the scope of this new financial scandal are still unfolding.

The Catholic Church's global annual expenses amount to more than $100 billion. In the U.S., Catholics now donate less than half as much per household as their Protestant counterparts, giving only around $6 billion per year. The Boston Archdiocese still reels from sex abuse scandals, and contributions to it have dropped by 43 percent to only around $8 million. Some archdioceses have been hit even harder; three have been forced into bankruptcy in anticipation of future settlements of sex-abuse cases. In Los Angeles alone, there are 550 pending cases. By 2006, the church had paid out around $1 billion for sex abuse cases going back several decades, and ongoing bills involving hundreds of offenders amount to hundreds of millions per year.

Between accusations of moral bankruptcy and the financial bankruptcy of some of its dioceses, the Catholic Church is experiencing its worst crisis since the death of Christ more than 2000 years ago.

About the Author

Janet Tavakoli is the bestselling author of several non-fiction finance books. *Structured Finance & Collateralized Debt Obligations* (John Wiley & Sons, 2003, 2008), and *Credit Derivatives* (Wiley, 1998, 2001), both global bestsellers in their respective fields, revealed abuses in the global financial markets. In *Dear Mr. Buffett: What An Investor Learns 1,269 Miles from Wall Street*, (Wiley 2009), she reveals the cronies and culprits responsible for the global financial crisis. *Archangels: Rise of the Jesuits*, is her fiction debut.

Ms. Tavakoli is the founder and president of Tavakoli Structured Finance, Inc. (TSF), a Chicago-based consulting firm established in 2003 for clients including financial institutions, institutional investors, and hedge funds.

She is a world-renowned author and speaker on derivative products and securities with more than 22 years of experience structuring, trading and selling derivatives and structured products while working for global Wall Street firms in New York and London.

The University of Chicago profiled her as "Structured Success," and *Business Week* as "The Cassandra of Credit Derivatives." The International Monetary Fund, the Federal Reserve Bank, the Office of the Comptroller of the Currency, and the Securities and Exchange

Commission have tapped her expertise in various forums.

Ms. Tavakoli is frequently published and quoted in financial journals, including *The Wall Street Journal, The Financial Times, New York Times, The Economist, Business Week, Fortune, Global Risk Review, RISK, IDD, Chicago Tribune, Los Angeles Times, LIPPER HedgeWorld, Asset Securitization Report, Journal of Structured Finance, Investor Dealers' Digest, International Securitization Report, Bloomberg News, Bloomberg/Business Week Magazine, Credit, Derivatives Week, TheStreet.com, and Finance World*.

Frequent television appearances include CBS's *60 Minutes,* CNN, C-Span, CNBC, BNN, *CBS Evening News,* Bloomberg TV, *First Business Morning News,* Fox, ABC, and BBC.

Ms. Tavakoli earned a Bachelor's degree in Chemical Engineering from the Illinois Institute of Technology and an MBA in Finance from the University of Chicago Graduate School of Business, now known as the Booth School of Business. She is a former adjunct associate professor of finance at the Booth School of Business where she taught "Derivatives: Futures, Forwards, Options and Swaps."

For further information please see: www.tavakolistructuredfinance.com

You've finished. Before you go...

Tweet/share that you finished this book.

Please write a brief customer review on Amazon or your favorite site for book lovers.

Janet Tavakoli's new nonfiction thriller, *Unveiled Threat: A Personal Experience of Fundamentalist Islam and the Roots of Terrorism* is available on Amazon.

Made in the USA
San Bernardino, CA
10 December 2014